THE ADVENTURES OF THREE OLD GEEZERS

Volume II

Up, Up and Away

Richard Perron

Richard Perron (signature)

ISBN 10: 1720309272
ISBN 13: 978-1720309277

ACKNOWLEDGMENTS

Here it is, Volume II. This sequel was only possible with the help of Nora Butler. Her editing skills and ability to take my ideas and expand on them enabled me to get them on paper. Her talents as an artist gave birth to the cover, and I am very thankful. I would also like to thank Shawn Merschdorf Kirby for her technical expertise and her proofreading skill. Her ability to navigate the computer world, of which I am a dinosaur, was invaluable in putting this book together. Last but not least, I would like to thank Frank and Bill for hanging in there.

In memory of Pat Causey

1951-2009

Lived thirty years in Alaska

overlooking the Matanuska Glacier.

A true mountain man if there ever was one.

CHAPTER 1

Here I am again, a few months after our last adventure, heading to Bad Ass Coffee to meet up with Frank and Bill for our early morning chat. It's the Three Old Geezers again. Frank, the retired hot dog king from New Hampshire. Bill, the retired hippy artist from Naples. And me, the retired former head shop owner, plant shop and greenhouse owner, musician, florist, charter boat captain, detailing guru, and last but not least, novelist. We're a real trio.

The sun is just rising, and the clouds are painted in deep orange and yellow. It's only May but feels more like a summer morning and a perfect morning for an epiphany. It's warm, and the scent of jasmine is wafting through the moisture-laden tropical air. Before long I can feel the first drop of perspiration sliding down the side of my face. It seems nothing ever changes. I have déjà vu. I know I've been here before, in fact, a thousand times.

All the snowbirds have gone back up north. Michigan, Illinois, and just about every other state in the Midwest and the northeast above the Mason-Dixon line is filled back up with Q-tips, as some people call the retired white-haired older folks down here. There's hardly any traffic on the roads now. You can ride a bicycle or scooter around without the fear of some ninety-year-old in their Rolls Royce making you their latest hood ornament as they fly through a stop sign oblivious to anything and anyone around them. There are also many people driving battery-powered cars, and you just can't hear them coming, not to mention the tourists who have no idea where they're going, their eyes on everything but the road. I always bike or walk facing traffic. I don't like them sneaking up behind me.

The first time I came down here was twenty-five years ago, in the month of November. I wondered what all the roads were for. You could roll a bowling ball down Fifth Avenue, the main street in Olde Naples, and not hit anyone. It soon became apparent that all these roads were barely enough to handle the avalanche of snowbirds that descended on Naples beginning right after Christmas and lasting until Easter. Even today, the road building goes on nonstop, trying to keep up with the retiring baby boomers moving south for good, or just to escape the winters. I guess all this growth is going to go on for a long time. Or, at least until they run out of baby boomers. Whenever that happens, the real estate prices are bound to suffer. Supply and demand, that's what it's all about. Many people bought a house in Olde Naples a few years ago for two hundred thousand dollars, and in a very short time, the house was worth a million. That doesn't happen in many cities. In 2008, when the financial crisis hit, property values dropped by half. If you're one of the "one percenters" it probably doesn't make much of a dent in your lifestyle, but for ordinary folk, it can be devastating.

A lot of people who bought houses in 2007 found themselves living in a house worth half as much. From 2002 to 2007 bankers were loaning money to practically anyone who could walk. Thousands of people got in over their heads. Gotta have stuff, doesn't matter if you can afford it or not, and the bankers were more than willing to loan the money. I don't know all the details, and I'm not sure if anyone really knows how it all works. Lots of shit hit the fan, and thousands of people lost their houses. Foreclosures were everywhere. I had a friend who bought a condo in a brand new twenty-story condominium in North Naples just as the economy went south. He ended up being the only one living in the building. No one else bought one. Buyer beware, that's the bottom line.

Today the boys and I are going to discuss plans for a fishing and camping trip. We need to have something exciting to keep us occupied. Our plan is to take Bill's boat and spend three days camping in the Ten Thousand Islands and to discuss options for our next big adventure. The time is getting closer for us to take off again and do something crazy.

CHAPTER 2

As I round the corner of 12th Avenue South onto Third Street, sure enough, Frank and Bill are sitting outside in front of Bad Ass Coffee. Frank is blowing perfect smoke rings from his cigar into the calm, dense air, and Bill is reading the Naples Daily News. Nothing seems to change. I've tried to get Bill to quit reading the newspaper, but to no avail. I don't really mind, as long as he keeps what he reads to himself. I just can't stand hearing all the negative crap, which I don't believe anyway, and besides, I really don't give a shit. Television and the newspapers are like a heroin addiction, just as bad for you and maybe even tougher to break. Bill, reading the paper and commenting on it, is just like religious people trying to convince me that their religious beliefs are the only way to go.

Believe what you want but leave me out of it. If you were born in India you're a Hindu, Israel makes you a Jew, if your parents are Baptist, you're a Baptist, if your parents are Catholic, so are you, and if you were born to a Muslim family, then you're a Muslim; Utah, you're a Mormon, and there are a hundred other views. So, who's right? Everybody or nobody? You got me!

Over forty percent of Christians in the United States think Jesus is coming back in their lifetime. Armageddon will be upon us, and only the believers will be saved, and the rest will rot in hell. I just don't know what to think about it all. I do believe that something more significant than me is running the show. I know that nobody, including biologists and scientists, is even close to understanding what's really going on; they don't even have the slightest idea what consciousness is. So, I shy away from conversations about politics and religion.

As soon as they see me, I'm hailed in the usual fashion," Hey Captain, see you're still breathing!" and I retort in the usual, "No money down, and twenty-five years to pay." I head right inside to get my tree hugger's breakfast.

I've changed my regular bagel and cream cheese routine. Now it's some kind of organic, gluten-free muffin with no preservatives or additives. In the last few months, I've gone Paleo. If you're not familiar with the term, it's a way of eating. Short for Paleolithic. It means eating like a caveman. No pasta, dairy, potatoes, rice, bread or anything with preservatives, or other additives. My friend NB got me into this new way of eating, and I've come to like it. Coffee without cream and sugar, imagine that. It's difficult in the beginning, but you soon get used to it, and if you go back to what you originally ate, it usually doesn't taste good. Most of it is too sweet. No milk, cream or sugar bowl in the house. I eat a lot of fruit and vegetables, bacon and eggs, meat, chicken, and fish. I've gone from 175 pounds to 155, and I feel light as a feather. This has all been lost on Frank and Bill.

I still walk with my four-pound weights every morning without fail. I still go down by the Naples Yacht Club, and sometimes come across the watchman patrolling the docks. It's fun to see him and know that I have a secret about the club that he'll never be privy to.

I've tried to get the boys on the tennis courts, which I've done a couple of times, but I guess it's not their thing. They're both like a fish out of water.

Bill still walks a bit, which he calls exercise, but you could get as much exercise as Bill does just walking to the bathroom. He can't free himself from his chocolate cake and other bad eating habits. Bill would rather be cruising around on his boat and doing a little fishing. I don't bug him that much about it, it's his body and his life, and he can do whatever he wants.

Frank keeps busy doing a few odd jobs around town even though he has a lot of money. It's important to have something to do. I'm still into my usual exercise routine. I would like these guys to be around for a few more adventures before our yardsticks of life run out.

As far as our finances go, we still have close to three million dollars between us, our reward for saving the rich guy and his family. That's enough to get us into serious trouble. We've thrown a few ideas around, and hopefully this weekend we can zero in.

When I came out, I sat next to Frank, who as you remember, was the hot dog king of the northeast. Before retiring, he ran a hot dog cart for many years in New Hampshire and made a damn good living. Actually, I think he had several hot dog carts. Being a cash business is always a plus. I bet the IRS wasn't privy to all those hot dogs Frank sold.

I started this morning's conversation by asking, "So, what do you old geezers think? Are we going to take your boat Bill and get out of town?"

Two thumbs up was all it took. After a few minutes of silently thinking about where we might like to go, we all decided to spend this Friday, Saturday, and Sunday in the Ten Thousand Islands. I wanted to go to Flamingo in Florida's Everglades National Park. It's as far south in the Florida mainland as you can go, but Bill reminded me that as soon as we get out of the truck, we would be covered in thick black clouds of mosquitos. It didn't take much to convince me that location would be a poor choice.

CHAPTER 3

It's called the Ten Thousand Islands because there's a shitload of islands. *Duh!* I don't believe there are *that* many, but ten thousand does sound impressive. I suspect nobody knows just how many there really are. It's a vast area of small islands, made up mostly of mangrove trees, bordering on Everglades National Park.

Mangrove trees are also called walking trees. They can live in salt water through a process known as reverse osmosis. Their roots can turn salt water into fresh water. They grow about as tall as their elaborate root system grows down which is about fifteen feet. As the trees mature they make seed pods, which eventually drop in the water and float off to make more mangrove trees, and the beginnings of a new island. The roots extend above the water line as well as below, rendering them almost impossible to walk on. In the right location the roots gather up sand and silt, and you end up with a few of the islands having a bit of a beach shoreline and a few sandy clearings.

The surrounding water is a beautiful blue-green color, rather shallow, only a few feet deep at most and offers some of the best fishing in Florida. Redfish, snook, sea trout, pompano, tarpon, snapper, and many other species abound, including the alligator and some crocodiles.

The shallow protected water beneath the mangrove roots offers protection and hiding places for the young fish from predators. In fact, this is where many of the species of fish in the Gulf of Mexico begin their life cycles before heading out to deeper water. Fortunately for us, these small fish attract the predators, and that's what we're after.

We're going to take Bill's boat, some camping gear, and according to Bill, we're going to stay on one of the more hospitable islands which has a small sandy shoreline and a clearing suitable to pitch a tent. We'll launch the boat a few miles south of Naples in Chokoloskee, a small fishing village, which is connected by a causeway to Everglades City, another small village full of stilt homes and fishing camps.

These are little towns located at the beginning of the Ten Thousand Islands, and anglers from all over the country and the world come here to fish. Even presidents have come here to try their luck.

You need to be cautious boating in this area. It's essential to know where you're going. There aren't any markers to indicate where you are. One mangrove island looks pretty much like the rest, and with thousands upon thousands of acres, it's easy to get lost. Bill has been there a lot of times and knows his way around pretty well, but being Bill, you can never be entirely sure he knows what he's doing.

So, Friday morning we'll be on our way for another Old Geezer adventure. We have today and tomorrow to get ready. I finished my tree hugger breakfast, shot the breeze for a few minutes with the boys and left to go on my daily walk. Have to keep in shape for our next adventure, whatever it will be. I also have to go to Ace Hardware to pick up a few things for our trip. I'll see the boys one more time before we leave tomorrow morning, as usual, at Bad Ass Coffee.

CHAPTER 4

It's Friday, and everything is packed in Bill's truck for our weekend getaway into the Ten Thousand Islands. We have a rather large new tent which the three of us will be sharing, and all of the equipment which goes along with a successful camping trip. We have a stove, lanterns, utensils, dishes, sleeping bags, fishing gear, folding chairs, rum, and a little pot that Bill wanted to bring along. For medicinal purposes of course. We're also bringing a few things to grill, like hamburgers, hot dogs, (which Frank wouldn't go anywhere without), and a couple of steaks. Without a doubt, we're bringing too much stuff. I made sure we didn't forget the bug spray!

We're hoping to catch some fish, but you can never depend on the fishing being good. Best to be prepared. Of course, I'm bringing my .357, and I've borrowed an AK-47, and a .22 pistol from one of my friends, just to do a little target practice. Lots of alligators and crocodiles roaming about, and this time of year they're breeding, not too friendly, and they can get a little edgy. We may have to put a little fear into one of them.

You probably haven't heard too much about the Burmese Pythons roaming out of control in the Everglades. Maybe as many as a hundred thousand of them slithering about, and some twenty feet long. They've been known to swallow alligators whole, and even deer. A lot of people in Miami bought them from exotic pet shops before they became illegal to sell. A cute little snake, until they begin to grow like a weed and get too big, too expensive to feed, and too scary to handle. That's when their owners decided to get rid of them by letting them loose in the Everglades. During Hurricane Andrew, which leveled a lot of southeast Florida, many pythons escaped from homes, zoos and nature parks that were destroyed. The government sends people out now to hunt them down and pays for their capture, but they're almost impossible to find. They are stealthy and can swim in both salt and freshwater. The python infestation has become a real problem. They're devouring the local wildlife, and when the food runs out, they'll be heading into neighborhoods.

People tend to freak out about these things, and in Naples, the powers-that-be don't want anyone to hear about an invasion of snakes, so you don't read much about it in the paper, in fact, whatever happens that doesn't reflect well on Naples usually doesn't appear in print. One of the finer restaurants was robbed at gunpoint, and the staff was locked in the meat cooler. Not newsworthy. Everything has to appear perfect. Don't want to upset the wealthy, and the Chamber of Commerce certainly doesn't want anyone to think twice about visiting or moving to Naples.

CHAPTER 5

We left early, right after our morning coffee at Bad Ass, and drove south on Route US 41, into the Ten Thousand Islands. There really isn't that much to see along the way. Mangrove trees line one side of the road, and the other side is grasslands as far as you can see. The Everglades is also called the "river of grass." It looks like the African Savannah and appears to be solid ground, but you would sink up to your knees or more if you tried to walk into it.

Locals in the area get around in swamp buggies, which are homemade contraptions with powerful motors and huge tires, with a frame built three or four feet off the ground for clearance. With this configuration, they don't get bogged down in the mucky soil. There are swamp buggy races held every year in Naples. They race in a drag street mode in three feet of mud. The event is even shown on Wide World of Sports, and for the finale, the winner gets to grab hold of the Swamp Buggy Queen, dressed in her gown, and jump into a three-foot-deep pit of muddy water. Sound like fun? It's basically a weekend of unrestrained redneck joy.

On our way, we drove past the smallest post office in the country. It's about the size of a small bathroom, and a tourist stop for photo ops.

Not a lot of people live in this desolate area. It's not very hospitable with its trillions of mosquitoes, hot and sticky weather, and alligators everywhere. You have to have a fence around your house to keep the gators out. Nothing worse than coming out in the morning with your coffee or coming home at night and being greeted by a big hungry gator.

There are little Indian villages all along the highway. Small compounds of Miccosukees and Seminoles that are federally recognized as Native Americans. Their houses are called "chickees," which is Spanish for house. The roofs are made of the fronds from cabbage palms, a native palm tree. Chickee huts have become popular around outdoor bars and pool areas. They're attractive, long-lasting, and indicative of the area. The only problem is, if you want one, or need one repaired, the Indians are the only ones allowed to do the work. Like it or not, it's the law.

Not far down the road is Big Dick's Master Bait & Tackle and Airboat Tours. Airboats are another way to get around in this part of the world. They are flat bottomed, made out of aluminum, about twelve feet long, six feet wide and generally carry six people, although there are larger ones carrying twenty, and smaller ones carrying only two. The passengers sit in the front, and the Captain sits on an elevated aluminum platform in back of them. Behind him is a big V-8 engine which powers an airplane propeller encased in an aluminum cage. They're very loud and fast. A stripped-down racing model can go one hundred thirty miles per hour, but the tour models probably don't go much more than twenty-five or thirty, which on the water, still seems mighty fast. Because of their shallow draft they can speed along on a few inches of water. In fact, they can maneuver where there isn't any water at all.

The tours may include sightings of birds, which don't tend to hang around when something that loud is in the area. They may run into a raccoon or two, who somehow learn to survive around some of the mangrove trees, using their root system as a highway. Of course, the most exciting sighting of all is an alligator. Generally, you don't see much wildlife. The ride itself is the big thrill.

I heard about a trip from hell on one of those machines. The airboat captains sometimes feed the alligators to keep them in the area for the tourist's entertainment. Feeding alligators is strictly forbidden, as it keeps the gators dependent on humans for their food.

In this particular case, the captain was leaning over the side with a dead fish in one hand patting the water and trying to entice some nearby alligator to come over for a snack. Without notice, an unseen alligator lunged up from below and grabbed his hand, spun over and tore his hand from his arm. I can only imagine the scene, blood flying everywhere, tourists screaming, the captain howling in shock and pain. In all the panic he was somehow able to retain his torn off hand and drive the airboat back to the dock one-handed. He made it to the hospital, hand in tow, but unfortunately, doctors were unable to reattach it. He was charged with illegally feeding an alligator. I don't think he was fined. The authorities felt he had already received enough punishment. The captain was lucky and survived, minus one hand and one fake Rolex. The suspect alligator didn't fare so well. He was hunted down and killed. How's that for justice? Unless you're on some crazy trip like that one, you don't really see much on an airboat tour. It's not like Mutual of Omaha's Wild Kingdom.

We did stop in Everglades City for a few minutes to see these crazy guys wrestling alligators. It seems like there ought to be a safer way to make a living than sticking your hand or head in an alligator's mouth. The tourists suck it up though, and I suppose these guys make out pretty good, except for maybe losing a finger once in a while. Truth is, alligators are not as dangerous as most people think. To get on their ugly side, you have to be in the wrong place at the wrong time. These guys obviously know what they're doing.

There are lots of misconceptions about the dangers of living in Florida. More people worldwide are killed by falling coconuts than by alligator or shark attacks. If you swim in New Smyrna Beach, Florida, you will definitely be within ten feet of a shark, but your chance of being bitten by one is almost zero.

So don't worry, be happy!

CHAPTER 6

We soon had enough of alligator wrestling and made our way to the boat launch in Chokoloskee, just down the road apiece. It didn't take but a few minutes to launch the boat and put all our stuff on board. Bill parked the truck and trailer, and we were on our way.

It was about thirty miles to our destination. Bill had a beautiful twenty-one foot fiberglass flats boat, powered by a 300 horsepower Evinrude outboard. Fifty miles an hour was a piece of cake as long as it wasn't rough on the water.

Flats boats operate best in areas of shallow water called flats. *Duh*. Obviously, that's where the name comes from. These boats have a flat bottom and draw very little water, which enables them to travel where most other boats with V-shaped bottoms can't go. Those types of vessels are used mostly for offshore cruising or fishing in deeper water. Today the water was flat as a pancake. I knew we were going to fly.

Bill put the pedal to the metal, so to speak, and we were off like a bat out of hell. In a short amount of time, I had no idea where we were, or how to get back. Bill was resolute in the fact that he knew exactly where we were and how to get back. We saw just one other boat along the way. Usually this time of year you don't run into anyone out here.

About thirty miles from where we put in, we came to a small mangrove island with a lovely sandy beach and a small clearing. Sandy beaches and clearings weren't all that easy to find out here, but apparently, Bill knew of a few. We circled the island for a few minutes, looking for the best place to put ashore. Oddly enough, this particular island in the middle of nowhere sports a dilapidated old port-o-potty on one of its little clearings. I don't know who would be coming around to empty it, or when the last time it even *was* emptied. We'll probably just use the little shovel we brought and some toilet paper. This time we didn't forget the toilet paper, unlike our sailing adventure of last year. Anyway, I don't know what might be living behind that hinged door, and I have no intention of finding out.

We pulled the boat up on the sand and unloaded. It only took a few minutes. Setting up the tent was a different matter, which seemed to take forever. This was a new tent Bill had bought specially for this occasion, and if you have ever put up a tent for the first time, it's about the same as putting kids' Christmas presents together. You have to think like a mechanical engineer. After about a half hour of profuse sweating and swearing, we had the tent up. Everything else was a piece of cake. By mid-morning, we were all set up, and Bill took up his cast net and strolled slowly and quietly about the shallow water looking for some live bait. Greenbacks were what we wanted. Small shiners about four inches long, which are irresistible to snook, and other game fish in the area.

We were in luck. Bill's first cast was successful, and he was able to get a net full of greenbacks. He emptied the net into the bait well on the boat to keep them alive and kicking, and we loaded up with some water, a few snacks, some rum of course, and took off to do a little fishing.

It was a picture-perfect day with big puffy white clouds, blue sky, and a slight breeze. Except for one other boat, which we saw quite a few times, we were all alone.

Bill caught several undersize snook and one beautiful keeper. Frank and I caught a nice redfish each. I hooked onto a shark, which was fun, but too much work. After ten minutes of straining my muscles, I cut the line and let him go. He wasn't what we were fishing for.

Bill was lucky enough to catch a nice tarpon. Must have been four feet long and it leaped high and shimmied all over the place, its silver scales shining in the sunlight every time it jumped. You can't keep tarpon as they're a protected game fish. You can take one scale, however, and then you have to release them. If you're lucky enough to remove a scale, you can take that to a taxidermist, and they will make you a plastic replica. They're one of the most prized sportfish in the world to catch. They're not good to eat, but they jump like crazy and are a hell of a lot of fun to reel in.

It was an excellent start to our weekend. We went back to camp and cooked up our fish. We decided to take the boat out again in the very late afternoon, to watch the sunset where we would have a good view of the horizon and have a few rum drinks. It doesn't get much better than this.

CHAPTER 7

L ate in the day, we took the boat out again to a place where we could have an unobstructed view of the sunset. We made a few rum drinks and sat back hoping to see the "green flash," a phenomenon which occurs at the very last moment before the sun finally sets. When the atmospheric conditions are perfect, a green flash of light can be seen for a couple of seconds. As the final rays of sunlight enter the atmosphere, the light spectrum is broken down, and the last light to be seen is green. Some people say it's a myth, but I have seen it and photographed the phenomenon quite a few times, and it's pretty cool.

The best part of a sunset in Florida this time of the year is actually *after* the sun goes down. The vast clouds that build up off to the east over the Everglades light up in many hues of yellow, orange, pink, gray, red, and all tints in between, surrounded by several shades of blue. It's impossible to get tired of Florida sunsets.

Frank was sitting on the front of the boat in a swivel fishing chair. Bill was at the helm, and I was standing next to him. Frank suddenly spun sideways and pretty much at the same moment I heard a loud *crack!* - what sounded like a gunshot. Frank fell onto the deck and immediately I heard a bang on the boat and another rifle shot. Frank was screaming, and there were blood spots on the deck. It didn't take a second to figure out we were being shot at, and I yelled at the top of my lungs.

"Bill, hit it! Get us out of here!"
Bill slammed the throttle forward as far as it would go, and we took off like a bat out of hell. I crawled forward to where Frank was lying on the deck and saw that he was bleeding from his arm.

I yelled back at Bill, "Take us back to our campsite as fast as you can!"

We were flying along with only the prop in the water, and probably doing sixty miles an hour. I took my shirt off and wrapped it around Frank's arm. I could swear I heard another gunshot. I kept pressure on Frank's bicep. I could only hope he wasn't hurt too badly.

As soon as we got back to the campsite, I helped Frank out of the boat to check him out. He could walk and basically got out of the boat on his own power. I took his shirt off, and sure enough, he was wounded, but it was a huge relief to see that it was only a flesh wound. We had a first aid kit on board, and I did the best I could to patch him up. We had a couple of painkillers in the kit, and I gave him one, hoping to relieve whatever pain he was in. He was alright at the moment, but we had greater problems to deal with.

This was insane. Here we were out in the middle of nowhere, and someone was shooting at us!

I had an intuitive sense about what had just happened, and I knew some nasty business was about to ensue.

I asked Bill, "Do you have any idea what just happened?"

"Hell no! But something crazy just took place! What do you think we should do?"

Frank, sitting in the sand, said, "I think I know what happened, and it was no accident!"

We all quickly came to the same conclusion… that it had to have been one of those crazy bastards from Everglades City, who we had the encounter with in the Bahamas last year.

We hadn't been out in open water, and he could have easily fired on us from one of the nearby mangrove atolls.

"I think he's been stalking us and waiting for an opportunity to get even." I spoke calmly, although my mind was whirling. We were like sitting ducks on the water.

"So, what do you guys think we should do about this? It's too late now to think about leaving and heading back to the launch. We could get shot at again. We can wait until morning and head back, but there's no guarantee we won't get shot at then, either. I say we take this matter into our own hands. This is going to have a nasty ending for someone - hopefully not one of us! If we are right, and it is who we think it is, we need to put an end to this now!"

"Bill, do you think we can figure out where they are?"

He nodded. "Yeah. I know this area pretty well, and there aren't a lot of possibilities. Taking into consideration where we were watching the sunset, I've got a good idea where they are."

I asked Frank, "How do you feel? Do you want to stay behind? And do you think this is a bad idea to go after them?"

Frank put it all straight.

"I'm pissed! I'm the one who got shot, and I want payback! I'm with you guys if this is what you want to do, but I'll tell you we're digging a very deep hole. One we may never climb out of. If we do go after them, then it's either them or us - someone's not coming home! We don't have any idea how many there are, but I suspect there are at least two assholes and maybe more."

"Ok, I said. "Here's what I think we should do. We'll take the boat but only use the trolling motor. Otherwise, they'll hear us coming. Bill, do you think the electric motor will get us over there?"

He responded, "If they're where I think they are, we can do it. It may take a while, but it's possible."

"Okay. Then, Bill, you and I are going to carry the weapons. We're both ex-military. We've got the AK-47 and the .357 and quite a lot of rounds. Frank, we may need you also, and I know you would like to get back at these guys.

I'm not sure what our plan will be when we find them, but most likely we'll need all three of us to pull this off. We should leave in a couple of hours when it's really dark. I don't think they'll be expecting us and we want to get to them before they come looking for us. I wish it had never come down to this. I think it may be a battle to the end. Right now, I wish I had whacked those two assholes back in the Bahamas! Let's get together what we need. The guns and ammo… and I wish we had some of that black shoe polish."

Bill piped in, "I got some underwear, and it's black, we can pull 'em over our heads and cut out some holes for eyes, and I got three pairs, including the one I'm wearing now, but I'll use that one."

I said, "I hope the others are clean." We all laughed at that one, but we were soon to be in some serious shit and knew our smiles would be wiped from our faces real soon.

CHAPTER 8

We let a couple of hours go by. The boat was loaded with guns, ammo, and almost as important, bug spray. Mangrove islands turn into Bug City after dusk. The mosquitos and no-see-ums are nearly as thick as the Bentleys in Naples.

We pushed off about ten thirty. Bill was to be in charge of the .357, and I had the AK-47. Frank had the small .22 that we brought along. I wasn't sure what we'd do with Frank when we got there. We'd have to put a plan together when we had a better sense of the situation.

The moon was barely visible, shining a little light on the water. Just enough to see shapes and outlines, but we were grateful for that.

After about an hour of slow going, I could see in the distance the light from a campfire. I muttered quietly to Frank and Bill, "These guys - whoever they are - can't be all that bright. It's hard to believe they're not concerned that we might hunt them down, like the dogs they are."

The boys agreed.

We had to take a wide curve around the little island and approach from the north side, downwind from their position. Frank whispered, "It's getting scary."

We made our way around the far side of the island and found a small sandy break in the mangroves and beached the boat. Stealth was the order of the night, which meant as little talking as possible. Frank quietly reassured us that he could handle the boat if he had to, so our plan quickly developed.

Frank was to take the boat back around the island, getting as close as he could to the campfire without being seen. When the action began, he was to come toward us as fast as possible to help us out if we needed it. Hopefully, we would be alive when he got there.

Bill and I were going to somehow make our way over the mangrove roots to the other side of the island. We took as much ammo as we could carry, put on plenty of bug spray, and finally pulled Bill's black underwear over our faces.

CHAPTER 9

Frank took off silently with the boat to take up his position, and Bill and I, staying as low as possible, followed the narrow sandy area for thirty feet into the mangroves. The beach suddenly ended, and we had no choice but to walk on top of the mangrove tree roots, which was no easy matter. It's hard to describe what a tangled mass of mangrove tree roots looks like, and how it's almost impossible to walk through. It took us about an hour of painstaking slipping, sliding, and climbing before we reached another sandy area close to the other side of the island, about fifty yards from where we had started.

I could smell their campfire and hear some muffled chatter that I couldn't understand. We got within thirty feet, and I could finally see them, and sure enough, it was those two pieces of shit from the Bahamas that we had so much trouble with. I put my lips right on Bill's ear and said as quietly as possible, "I'm not sure how close we'll be able to get. When we get as close as we can without being discovered, we'll open fire. Make the shots count."

Bill nodded without saying a word.

The sandy area we were on widened out a bit and I motioned Bill to take the right side, and I would stay on the left. We got on our bellies and silently inched forward. We were able to get within twenty feet without being seen. The two assholes were sitting, one on each side of the fire. The older one had his back to us. Out of nowhere, a huge python snake slithered out in front of Bill. He let out a loud gasp which caught the attention of the assholes.

The older one cocked his head in our direction, and said to the younger asshole, "Did you just hear something?"

The goofy one with the tattoos said, "Yeah. I think so. Maybe it's a raccoon or an alligator."

The older one wasn't totally stupid and spun quickly around and grabbed his gun and looked right in our direction. All of a sudden, he screamed, "What the fuck!"

That's when I let off a round and shot him right in the chest, and he flew backward into the fire and then rolled off. The young guy leaped up, and Bill immediately shot three rounds off with the .357. The blasts were accurate and propelled the man backward ten feet right into the water. We jumped to our feet and ran towards them. The old man was reaching for his rifle, which I kicked out of the way, and Bill ran for the young punk.

I stood over the old redneck. Blood leaked out of his mouth, his breathing was raspy, and his eyes were glassy and sad. I said to him, as I took Bill's underwear off my face, "Remember me? You rednecks just don't know when to leave well enough alone. You couldn't be as dumb as you look, but you are. I told you I wouldn't be so kind the next time we met. This is the last time you fuck with these three old geezers." I shot him one more time right in the heart, and that was all she wrote.

Bill screamed, "Get over here quick!"

I ran over to where Bill was staring intently, pointing at the other asshole floating in the water. The moonlight had intensified, and I instantly saw what he was looking at. There was a giant alligator heading straight for the obviously dead asshole, and before you could say your name, the alligator had him in his mouth, rolling him over and over and thrashing about in the water. Then he slowly swam off with asshole number two in his jaws and disappeared into the darkness.

I stood still, in shock and amazement. *"Holy shit, Bill!* I've never seen anything like that! And I hope I never do again! That's the creepiest damn thing I've ever seen!"

Before Bill even had time to respond, Frank came around and beached our boat.

Frank, no longer trying to be so quiet, yelled excitedly. "Wow, I heard the gunshots, and came as fast as I could!" Frank got out of the boat and could easily see the white-haired dead man by the fire and instantly recognized him.

"That's him alright! I guess he got what he asked for! Was there more than one of 'em?"

"Yeah, there were two. And number two is dinner."

I recounted to Frank what had happened. His jaw dropped, and he shook his head in disbelief when I told him about the gator. He looked at Bill and then back at me several times in amazement.

As much as we were all relieved, we knew we still had a problem on our hands, which was *what to do with the dead guy lying next to the campfire.* We decided not to bury him because undoubtedly somehow, someone would find him. It was just too risky that the body might be uncovered by the tide or an animal. We could throw him in the water and expect he would become dinner like his buddy. We decided on the latter. We pulled him into the water and hoped that our alligator friend or a shark would come along and take him for a ride. We also had to do something with their gear and of course the boat, and it all had to be done right away!

CHAPTER 10

After a short discussion, we decided to pack all their shit up and put it on their boat. I would drive the redneck's boat back to our campsite and follow Frank and Bill in Bill's boat. We also discussed calling the authorities, but who would believe our crazy story about the Bahamas, and what had happened here. We dismissed that idea right away.

Tomorrow, before sunrise we will take their boat twenty miles out into the Gulf of Mexico, put a few holes in it, and sink it along with the rest of their stuff. We'll keep their guns. No sense in throwing them away, they probably weren't registered anyway.

We knew this whole experience could eventually come back to haunt us and bring us many years of bullshit. We had to just continue on and hope for the best. After all, we didn't ask to be put in this situation.

I said laughingly to Frank and Bill, "At least we won't run into those assholes again, unless we eat the wrong alligator nuggets. I, for one, am not planning ever to eat alligator nuggets again." For some reason, I always think of something funny to say when there's nothing humorous at all. Must be a personality flaw.

We put out what was left of their campfire and tried to make the area look like no one had been there for a long time. We grabbed everything we could find, loaded it in the assholes' boat, and headed back to our campsite.

Three old geezers, and *another* stolen boat.

Upon returning to our site, it didn't take long to get out the rum, and the three of us sat drinking, mostly in silence. Frank had his worried look on, smoking a cigar and blowing his smoke rings into the night air while rubbing his arm. Bill was just staring off into the darkness. We were thinking about a hundred different scenarios, and how many of them could be the end of the Three Old Geezers' Adventures.

We rose early, about four a.m. I'm not sure any of us slept at all. We had to get this over with as quickly as possible. We agreed that I would drive the asshole's boat, and Frank and Bill would follow in Bill's boat.

It was a calm morning, thank heaven. The gulf was flat as glass. We left just as it was getting light. We put the pedal to the metal and went as fast as we could. When we reached a spot about twenty miles out, we came alongside each other, and I climbed over to Bill's boat. We all put earplugs in our ears, which we had brought along with us since we had planned to do some target practicing.

I learned a few years ago that you should never fire a weapon on a boat if you ever want to hear anything again. The water transforms the boat you happen to be sitting on into a giant megaphone. My ears are still ringing - years after firing my .357 on a boat without wearing earplugs. I played piano back then, and from middle C - which is basically the middle of the keyboard - to the highest note on the piano everything sounded the same. Ding, ding, ding. It took a couple of years before I could distinguish the different sounds on the high end. Even to this day the top ten or twelve notes all sound the same. So, I'm very cautious now.

I took my .357 and fired six rounds into the bottom of the boat, reloaded and fired six more. The boat immediately started taking on water, and in just a few minutes it disappeared under the surface, hopefully never to be found.

We made our way back to our spot as fast as we could without much conversation. We quickly packed up and headed back to the boat ramp. Our immediate plan was to get home, lay low, and maybe leave town for a while. It just might be time for the next big adventure, although it felt like we just had one!

Luckily, we didn't see anyone at the boat ramp. We loaded the boat on the trailer and took off. When we got back to Naples, we split up quickly and decided to meet at Bad Ass Coffee the next morning, as usual.

CHAPTER 11

Here we are at Bad Ass Coffee again. Seven o'clock in the morning, and we're pretty quiet, and a bit nervous. Something has to be done, and we know it. We can't just sit around, anxiously wondering what the consequences might be, if any, to our latest actions.

Frank with his worried look muttered, "We have to think about this. If they find those dead assholes, we could be in big trouble. I doubt anyone will ever find the one that got taken for a ride with the alligator, but the old man may be floating around out there for quite a while. Maybe we should have weighted him down, so he'd sink. Somebody could find him, and it may come back on us."

I had a sudden thought. "Bill, do you think Julie was still in touch with that guy?" (If you recall, Julie is Bill's wife who we ran into in the Bahamas, and then rescued from the two rednecks that we just shot and killed in the Ten Thousand Islands.)

Bill replied, "I don't know, she has been acting a little strange lately - not that that's unusual. Maybe she does know something, and she's keeping it to herself. But, after what happened in the Bahamas I really doubt she would have anything to do with those assholes again."

I agreed. "You're probably right. There's no way she would get involved again. She might have hooked up with somebody else, but not those guys again. And for your sake, I hope it's not somebody else either!"

Bill, with a clouded face, grumbled. "I really don't give a shit these days. Whatever will be will be. I can survive no matter what. I could live in a hole in a tree if I had to and be happy. In fact, I think all we're doing won't mean shit before too long. It will all just be like a pee hole in the snow or a fart in the wind. It just won't matter. I don't mean to be sounding all depressed, but reality is what it is, and I still believe we better get it while we can."

"I know where you're coming from," I said, "but we have to deal with the present situation. I don't think those guys got any information from Julie about our little fishing trip. I think they were probably stalking us and we just weren't aware of it, or by some crazy twist of fate they just happened to be out there at the same time we were and thought they had an opportunity they couldn't pass up. I guess we'll never know. Never in my wildest dreams did I ever think we would see those two again. It's really a small world."

Frank nodded in agreement. "At least we know we won't be running into them again, unless, as you said, we eat the wrong alligator nuggets." We all smiled, despite knowing there wasn't any real humor in the situation.

"You know Frank," I said quietly, "I keep thinking about your ability to fly a plane. I have a friend who owns an airplane maintenance business at the airport. He may be able to fix us up with a plane we can borrow for a few weeks or months. It's a long shot, but it might be worth a try."

It's the same situation with small private planes as it is with boats in Naples. When the rich depart, they frequently leave both behind.

We may not be able to steal one, but with a little bit of money, we may be able to borrow one, if you know what I mean.

I continued with my idea. "He's a very good friend of mine. We use to ride Harley Davidson's together. I'm sure he'd be interested in making some extra money. Between the three of us, we have lots of money, and for twenty, thirty maybe forty thousand dollars he might hook us up."

Frank said, "Hell yeah! I'm willing to give it a shot. What about you Bill?"

Bill rolled his eyes and said somewhat unconvincingly, "I'm with you. Whatever you guys think is best. If we take off for parts unknown why don't we just buy a plane ticket? Besides, where are we going to go?"

"Listen, Bill, we could buy plane tickets, or we could even afford to buy our own plane for that matter, but what fun would that be?"

Frank excitedly piped in, "I just thought of something! I have a cousin who lives in Alaska on the side of a mountain, overlooking a big glacier. He built his cabin from scratch. It's pretty isolated - there's nobody around for miles. I went there a few years ago to visit him. Lots of hunting and fishing. We could possibly fly all the way up there and hang out with the bears and salmon for a few weeks or months, and hopefully, things will blow over down here. He lives there year-round, and I'll bet he would love some company. Whenever I need to get in touch with him, I have a number to call, and I leave a message, and someone delivers it to him. I'm sure he would like to see us, and of course, he's as crazy as we are."

I asked Frank, "Do you think you can fly that far and get us there alive?"

Frank with his worried look answered, "I wouldn't bet all our money on it, but I am instrument rated, and I can fly a twin engine. All my licenses are up to date, so I'm ready to go anytime."

"Okay, then, I'm going to talk to my friend at the airport this afternoon and see what kind of deal we can work out, if any. Frank, you try to get in touch with your cousin up in Alaska. I'll see you guys again tomorrow morning, same time, same place."

I thought to myself...*well, what the hell...we have to do something, and it might as well be something crazy.*

That attitude is right up our alley. I'm going to cross my fingers and hope for the best.

CHAPTER 12

Naples Airport is located just on the outskirts of the city. It's a small airport, only non-commercial flights, but for its size and designation, it's one of the busiest in the country. There's room for over two hundred private jets, not to mention many smaller aircraft. There are planes continually flying in and out, but Fridays and Sundays are the busiest. During season, one jet lands every three minutes on Friday, and one takes off every three minutes on Sunday. I've heard they're mostly corporate jets. At least a hundred of the Fortune 500 CEO's have a home in Naples. Somebody's making a *lot* of money!

There's a viewing stand at the end of the runway, and lots of people go there to sit on the benches, watching the comings and goings. Fifty million dollar jets, one after another.

When these influential people land, there are a couple of uniformed workers who ride out on big golf carts to greet them and give them a ride over to the terminal. It's the red-carpet treatment.

There has been an effort in the past, by local residents who don't own multi-million-dollar jets, to have the airport relocated. It encompasses a large area of valuable land within the city, which could be used for the benefit of all the population. One solution would be to have these wealthy individuals land in Fort Myers, which is about 35 miles north of Naples, and drive down, but the rich have so much money and influence that moving the airport would most likely never happen.

I pulled off Airport Road onto a narrow gravel road that led to the back of my friend's hangar. I got out of the car, walked to the edge of the hangar, stuck my head inside and yelled, "Hey George!"

The sound echoed and bounced off the giant metal walls. George was up on a ladder, bent over working on the engine of a small airplane. Startled, he stood up, banged his head on the cowling and almost fell off the ladder. He screamed, "Jesus Christ do you have to do that every time you stop by? Someday I'm going to fall and break my fucking neck!"

"Sorry George, just making sure you're still awake! I've stopped by to have a little private conversation. I have a deal you might be interested in."

"Ok," he said, climbing down from his ladder. "Let's go into my office but keep your voice down!"

We walked over to his small office located in the back corner. It was surrounded by pieces of metal and various engine parts, and I couldn't make out what any of them were. I was never much of a mechanic.

Inside, there was the overwhelming odor of a combination of oil, grease, and gasoline. I sat down in an old leather chair which had seen one too many asses and should be in a dumpster somewhere. George was wiping his hands with a dirty rag as he sat in an old swivel chair which should have been discarded at the same time as the one I was sitting in. The surface of his banged-up gray metal desk was covered with more metal parts, pieces of leather and oil-soaked rags.

I inquired of George, "Do you even know what all this crap is?"

"Of course, I know what it is," he said impatiently. He got right to the point. "So, what's so important that you need to talk to me in private about?"

"Well, I've got a deal for you. I can't give you all the details of what's led up to the request I'm about to make. Let's just say I don't want to get you involved any more than you have to be. To put it simply, my two buddies and I need to get out of town for a while. We need a plane to use for maybe two or three months. I thought you might know of one that we could "borrow," so to speak, and return without anyone being the wiser."

George leaned forward with his elbows on the desk and looked at me with raised eyebrows. "Are you crazy? You can't get away with shit like that anymore! People keep track of everything. And, even if that wasn't the case, do any of you guys even have a pilot license?"

I explained that my friend Frank was certified for twin-engine planes and had all the required papers. I also threw in the fact that we were willing to pay a fair amount of money for the privilege. I had heard through the grapevine that George's wife was in trouble. She was on the verge of being arrested for embezzling escrow money from real estate deals, along with her lawyer. Everyone thought it strange that George and his wife had a beautiful home on the bay, two Mercedes, and a couple of very expensive boats. In a way, it was just like the drug smuggling fishermen from Everglades City. No money in fishing, but everyone had a new truck and a Rolex watch. Just doesn't add up. Two plus two doesn't equal five.

CHAPTER 13

I didn't bother mentioning to George that this was not my first rodeo in borrowing airplanes. I'd had a bit of experience at it. When I was only fifteen, in my hometown of Concord, New Hampshire, I had a good buddy named Doug, who worked at the local airport in Concord. Instead of getting paychecks, Doug preferred to be compensated in flight lessons, and when he was sixteen, he got his private pilot's license. It was a tiny airport, nothing like the Naples Airport. At night, after everyone had left he would open up the hangar and roll out a Cessna. A couple of times I was goaded into going up with him and flying around for an hour or so, before bringing the plane back and returning it to the hangar. I can tell you it was pretty scary, and very exciting. We never did get caught for that, but we did get caught stealing the rental cars and driving them around. We just got a slap on the wrist for that prank. Kids will be kids. Today they would probably throw us in prison.

When I mentioned again, that we would be willing to pay, George seemed to lighten up some. "So, you said. Well, how much are you talking about?"

"We're willing to pay you twenty thousand dollars to compensate you for any risk you may take, and if something happens, you could always say the plane was stolen." I had started with the amount of twenty thousand dollars because I was pretty sure he was going to want a lot more than that. Lawyers cost a lot of money. I knew he wasn't stupid!

We both sat there in silence for a few minutes, and I could see his brain was operating on high. His eyes were moving from side to side, and I could almost hear his mental adding machine clacking away.

Finally, he said, "I have a plane that I take care of, which is owned by a very, very rich guy who's going to be in China for about six months. You may be able to get away with it, but twenty thousand bucks just doesn't cover it for my part in this. He looked me straight in the eye and said, "But forty thousand would seal the deal."

Before he could take another breath, I said, "It's a deal!!"

We shook hands, and that was that. He said I could have the airplane in a week, and that I was to bring Frank over soon, so they could talk and get acquainted with the plane and take it up for a test flight.

I quietly left and drove off with a smile on my face. Here we go again! Another adventure for the Three Old Geezers. I can't wait to tell the boys.

CHAPTER 14

I had a few errands to run before returning to my condo. It was about three o'clock when I got back, and as I rounded the corner I could see a cop car in front of my condo complex, and that was enough to send me into a tizzy. I didn't stop. I continued on, not even daring to look his way. Could they indeed have found out about those two assholes that fast, and tied us to the crime?

I called Bill and Frank to ask if anything suspicious had been going on for them. They hadn't noticed anything. Maybe I was just feeling paranoid.

I explained to them about going to the airport in a couple of days to check out the plane, and that Frank could take it for a test flight. Bill was still nervous about the idea; Frank was excited.

I waited a couple of hours, then headed back to the condo. No one was lurking about. I went inside and opened up a new bottle of Captain Morgan and had a couple of quick swigs.

I was exhausted and decided to stretch out for a while on the couch. I was wondering about what was going to happen in just a few days. Life can take some funny twists and turns. Just when you think all is well- POW! -right in the kisser. How can you plan on something like this? One minute you're fishing and the next you kill someone, and to top it off, you're taking a "borrowed" plane to Alaska. It just doesn't make any sense.

We're flying over the Gulf of Mexico when Frank apparently passes out, and the plane starts to fall. I scream at Frank, "Frank! Frank! Are you OK?" There's no answer, and I have to take control. Bill is yelling, "What's wrong with Frank? Is he dead?" I yell back, "I think so. Hold on tight and buckle up. We're going down!" Bill screams, "I'm getting out!" He opens the door and jumps. I continue down and down and crash into an oil platform. I fall out of the plane and roll off the oil platform into the Gulf of Mexico where I am soon being chased by an alligator.

I woke up in a sweat, my heart pounding away like a rock drummer, just in time to go meet the boys at Bad Ass.

CHAPTER 15

A few days passed before George called to say he was ready to take us up and check out Frank's pilot skills, and that we should meet him at the airport at about noon.

I was rounding the corner to Bad Ass, and sure enough, like clockwork, there were my two buddies. I went inside and got my usual tree hugger breakfast and came out and sat down. Bill was reading the Naples Daily News and barely looked up. There were no cheerful greetings this morning. Frank had that worried look and Bill, gripping the newspaper, began staring at the wall, apparently deep in thought.

I said, "So what's up? You guys look like you've seen a ghost."

Bill quickly replied, "Well, here it is, and I'm going to read it straight out of the paper." He looked around to see if anyone was listening.

He read, "Two Everglades City residents, Wilber Coombs and Junior Coxwell, have been reported missing somewhere in the Ten Thousand Islands. The two were last seen in Chokoloskee by a Fish and Game officer as they were launching their boat several days ago. Relatives say the two were going camping and fishing for a couple of days. The national park service has done some flyovers in the area, looking for any trace of the two men and their boat. So far, no signs or evidence has been reported. The search will continue for several more days. Anyone with any information, please call the local authorities."

Bill lowered the paper he'd been reading, and said in a low, raspy voice, "We definitely have information, but we won't be calling any authorities. In fact, I think we need to get the hell out of here."

I added that I wouldn't be a bit surprised if someone came to question us, but that we shouldn't get paranoid yet. Frank wanted to know more about the relatives that reported them missing. He thought there was a possibility that

Julie may have some information about the relatives.

"Listen, guys, not to change the subject, but I heard from George this morning. He wants to do a test flight at noon today, if possible. Then, maybe in a couple more days, we can fly out of here. What do you say we meet at my place later this morning and then head for the airport?"

It was scary to think that all this was happening because of those two assholes from Everglades City. *We were now being forced to take off on another adventure...* Sometimes all you need to start another adventure is to kill a couple of assholes, and off you go.

CHAPTER 16

At eleven thirty we met at my place. Bill had some interesting news, but first, he said he had to take a leak. I yelled at him as he headed to the bathroom. "Don't forget to sit down when you go; I don't want piss all over the place.

"Ok, ok, you don't have to remind me every time I'm here!"

My friend Bubba told me years ago that one reason women live longer than men is because they squat to pee. It may not seem natural, but when you think about it, it makes sense. A lifetime of standing all tensed up and peeing, when women calmly sit to do their business, shortens a man's life expectancy. It only stands to reason. The act of sitting also empties your bladder better, and it's a lot more sanitary.

Bill came back shortly and continued, "I talked to Julie for a few minutes at breakfast today. She'd read the newspaper and made a comment about the two lowlifes gone missing. She said she didn't know they had come back here, but that it was quite a coincidence that they went missing in the Ten Thousand Islands the same weekend we went fishing there. I agreed that it *was* strange. I also told her it was a huge area and highly unlikely that we would happen to run into those two dip-shits. I pretended to think it just odd to hear that they were crazy enough to return, after what had happened and what we told them *would* happen if we ever saw them again. Julie tried to impress upon me the fact that we might be prime suspects in an investigation if something suspicious happened to them. So, I told her it would be difficult to tie us in unless they found out about our misadventures with them in the Bahamas. I asked her if she had met any of their relatives. She told me she met a couple of cousins that lived in Goodland; a couple of crazy old coots living on an old sailboat."

I began feeling queasy, thinking about the possibility of the police somehow tying Julie in, and deciding to question her. What if she tells them about us going fishing at the same time, and our Caribbean history with those guys? That would not be good.

I decided that was paranoid thinking, and I said to Bill, "Well, yes, things could get messy, but I don't think Julie would be stupid enough to mention that to the police, and it's a little farfetched to think that the police would connect Julie to those two ding dongs. That only happens on TV. Now, let's get out of here and head for the airport."

On our way there we discussed what we might say if we were to have the misfortune of being questioned by the police before we left. We had no idea who the two assholes might have talked to before they went looking for us, or if it was just fate that they ran into us. I know they didn't speak to anyone *after* our encounter in the Ten Thousand Islands! They could have mentioned us to their cousins or someone else about our contact in the Bahamas, which would really put us on their radar. The best we could do is to deny everything. Those two probably have a lot of enemies wanting to do them harm. They weren't exactly a couple of boy scouts. We would just dumb up.

I told Bill that he should inform Julie as soon as possible about our plan to fly out to Frank's cousin's camp in Alaska and tell her that his cousin requested our help in rebuilding his camp after a big storm. "If she suggests that she wants to come along, you'll just have to tell her it's a guy thing and that we're flying up in a friend's plane and may be gone for a couple of months. Hopefully, she won't put up too much of a fuss."

We made it to the airport and George was waiting outside the hangar standing next to one of the most impressive planes I've ever seen. Smooth, white as snow, and sexier than a Victoria's Secret model. He explained that the plane was a Beechcraft Baron Fifty-Eight. Frank spoke right up. "I know about these. I've flown quite a few of 'em. They're a piece of cake. They almost fly by themselves."

I was very glad to hear that, and I'm sure George was too. We made our introductions, and everyone was ready to go.

CHAPTER 17

We boarded quickly. Bill and I got in the back, and Frank took the seat up front next to George. We sat for a moment before George started up the engines and you could just feel the power waiting to be released. George had a few things to say to the tower, and we quickly taxied out to the end of the runway. I could see the viewing stand off to my left where I've sat many times, sipping a Captain and coke, and watching the planes take off and land, but had never seen it from this position. I always wondered where all those planes were going, and what far-off worlds they were flying to.

We straightened out on the runway, and George revved the engines while keeping his foot on the brakes. You got the feeling you were in a slingshot just waiting to be catapulted down the runway. George asked Frank if he wanted to take it from the very beginning, and like a trooper, he gave a thumbs up.

In a few seconds Frank took the brakes off and gave it full throttle, and I was immediately pushed firmly back against my seat. Before I knew it, George said, "rotate," and up we went. I didn't know what rotate meant, but it sounded cool. We banked right and headed south over the Ten Thousand Islands - the scene of the crime.

I'm not particularly fond of flying. When I was young, maybe ten years old, my father belonged to the Civil Air Patrol. A civilian organization basically made up of wannabe fighter pilots, who were called into action to help out the professionals in search and rescue missions.

My dad had a pilot's license and had access to their plane. One day he offered to take me for a ride. The Civil Air Patrol in my hometown had an old two-seat Piper Cub which must have been manufactured shortly after the Wright Brothers first flight. It had a seat in the front and one in the back. The controls were simple, two foot pedals and a stick. You could see right through several small cracks in the floor. I'm not sure that bucket of nuts and bolts was even certified to fly. I remember that a man came out of the hangar and gave the prop a couple of twists and the engine started. We taxied out to the end of the runway, straightened out, and my father gave it the gas. The plane shook all over as it slowly made its way down the runway, seemingly unable to take off. We finally lifted off the ground. It took forever to get to whatever height we reached, which wasn't all that high but seemed so to me, and just as long to get down. That one flight traumatized me to the extent that I never really wanted to fly after that. To be honest, I don't really think it was that flight which gave me a fear of heights - it may have been the roller coaster my dad talked me into going on when I was maybe seven, or I could have just been *born* afraid of heights. I'll never know. I can't imagine being an eagle and scared of heights.

I flew with my buddy when we stole the plane from the airport, but it wasn't without white knuckles all the way. I have also flown a few times since then. When I was fifteen, and my pilot friend was sixteen, four of us flew from New Hampshire to the World's Fair in Flushing,

New York. That's another story. Sometimes flying is unavoidable, like when I was in the military, or going on vacations. I was never comfortable, and often my flying excursions were preceded with a valium and a Captain Morgan or two.

But this plane was different. It was like an immaculate high-end sports car. I felt safe, especially knowing there were two engines, although I wasn't interested in doing any fancy maneuvers.

Frank and George continued their conversation and Bill and I stared out the windows enjoying the view. We flew over the area of the Ten Thousand Islands where our shootout was, but of course, we couldn't make out anything on the ground. We did see a couple of Coast Guard helicopters flying around, and I was pretty sure what they were looking for.

Frank turned around to make sure we were buckled in. He said, "We're going to do a stall and recovery, so don't be scared." No sooner had he said that than I could see the nose of the plane go up, and a few seconds later the nose went down as my stomach went up. We quickly regained level flight, and it was over. I hoped they weren't going to do any crazy eights, or barrel roles.

I was starting to feel relaxed and comfortable. This was quite the piece of machinery. Frank was at the controls most of the time, and my respect for him was growing by the minute. We flew around for a couple of hours before Frank brought us in for a smooth, perfect landing. We taxied over to the hangar and quickly got out.

George was shaking Frank's hand apparently impressed with his aeronautical skills, and so was I. George said we could take off for Alaska anytime we wanted.

Frank had a lot of planning to do, as far as our flight plan went. He had to know how many miles we would cover each day and/or night. I wasn't too excited about flying at night, but I felt comfortable trusting Frank. I was prepared to do whatever he said. Before we left the airport, I suggested that we all get together tonight at my place, including Julie, and decide what we are going to say if questioned by the police.

We all agreed that we needed to be on the same page - *and the sooner, the better.*

CHAPTER 18

We were all sitting around my kitchen table. We knew there was a good chance we would be confronted by the police. How we handled the situation could mean the difference between going to prison or not.

I started off the conversation by saying, "Listen, guys, at some point we'll be approached by the cops, and the worst thing we can do is to deny we ever met those two assholes. If we deny it, we'll surely be suspects because I'll bet his cousins know all about us and will surely give them our names. I believe without a doubt the cousins know about Julie, and most likely what happened in the Islands. Julie, have you met them, and do you think they know anything?"

"I have met the cousins a couple of times, but I don't understand what you're worried about.

Did you guys have something to do with their disappearance?"

Now it gets sticky. We either keep Julie out of this, or we tell her everything. I decided we should not tell her what happened in the Ten Thousand Islands because that would incriminate her and make her a party to the crime. Also, since we are planning to leave town, it would be smart to have someone back home to keep us posted on any developments.

"Listen, Julie," I said. "We all know the history, and most likely someone is going to come and talk to us, and we feel it's best if we leave town for a while. Frank's cousin needs some help with his camp, and that's why we're flying up there. It would be helpful to have someone here to let us know what's going on. Someone loyal to us. I'm sure you'll never forget that we saved your life.

Another thing I'm worried about are the two cousins. I'm not sure what they know about anything, but they may think we had something to do with the disappearance of their relatives and decide to come after us, and we don't want that to be easy for them. It's best you don't know anything about what did or didn't happen in the islands. You don't know anything, and that's all there is to it."

I continued, "So let's leave it like this, Julie. You know nothing about the Ten Thousand Islands. If the cops ask about the Bahamas, you can tell them the truth about what happened there. No sense lying about it, that will only cause suspicion. The rest of us will do the same. Tell the truth about the Bahamas, and just say we went fishing the weekend they went missing. We didn't see or hear anything. It's a huge area, so it wouldn't be strange that we never saw them. I agree it's a little ironic that we would have been in the islands at the same time, but there's a lot of irony in life. It happens all the time. That doesn't make someone guilty. It's all circumstantial. I'm sure those two creeps had lots of enemies."

We all agreed, and that was that. In two days, we were flying out. If questioned, we all knew what to say.

We agreed to meet the next morning at Bad Ass Coffee, like nothing unusual was going on.

Suddenly my cell phone went off.

"Captain Richard here. Hello, Lieutenant. Yeah, yeah, I know them, they're friends of mine. Of course, we can talk with you. It might be a little awkward, but we'll all be at Bad Ass Coffee around nine tomorrow morning." Pause. "Sure, we'll meet you there, and you can talk to all of us at once. Nine o'clock. Ok, great, see you in the morning."

I hung up. "That was Lieutenant Jameson from the Collier County Sheriff's Office. He wanted to meet with us tonight, but I got him to agree to tomorrow morning at nine o'clock at Bad Ass Coffee. So here we go. Let's just all go home and take it easy. If we're cool about this, all will be fine. If you get nervous, just let me do the talking. Julie, you can be there if you want, because I'm sure they're going to get to you also, and you may have a message waiting for you when you get home. Keep in mind; we never did anything that wasn't forced upon us. So, for now, let's break up, and I'll see you all tomorrow."

Everybody left, and my mind was going round and round. Here I am, in a terrible situation, and I feel like a victim of circumstance. There's not much I can do about it. We could turn ourselves in and tell the truth, and just hope we don't end up with first-degree murder charges. I know there a lot of innocent people locked up, in fact, if you ask anyone in prison whether they're guilty or innocent, you know what the answer will be. I wasn't about to take a chance. I'm going to fight this to the end. I couldn't do anything but hope that tomorrow morning would go smoothly.

CHAPTER 19

We all arrived at Bad Ass Coffee at about eight am and took up our typical positions around the table. Me, with my healthy breakfast, Frank blowing smoke rings, Bill reading the newspaper, and Julie biting her nails and looking nervous.

I tried to calm things down.

"Look there's nothing to be worried about. All we have to do is answer their questions. We all know what happened in the Bahamas, so we'll tell it just like we remember it. As far as their disappearance goes, we are like the three monkeys, hear no evil, see no evil and speak no evil."

It was quiet around the table. Nobody had much to say. We were inside our own heads running our own scenarios about what was going to happen.

A car pulled up in front of the coffee shop, and we knew right away it was the cops. They were driving a nondescript car, with absolutely nothing extra on it, with a dull blue paint job. With all the fancy cars around this town, this one was plainly out of place. The front doors opened, and two guys got out. One was rather short, bald and chubby, with a round red face. He appeared a little unkept and was busy trying to tuck in his shirt which was half in and half out. I could tell he didn't like the heat, or the cheap dark suit he was wearing. It was a little tight. He most likely had put on some weight since he bought it. His partner was a better dresser. Not expensive clothes, but in good taste. His tie was colorful with some flowers on it, so I expected he had a sense of humor, but never take cops for granted. They're taught to look like they know less than they really do. He was also somewhat lean, like a runner, or biker. The chunky one was in his fifties, and the younger one was probably early forties.

There aren't many people at the coffee shop this time of year. Most everyone in this part of town has left for their summer homes up north, and it's too early for any of the British, or other tourists to be up and about. In other words, we were easy to spot.

They came right over to the outside eating area, and I quickly stood up as they approached.

"Lieutenant Jameson, I assume," I said quietly and firmly. "I'm the Captain, and these are my friends Frank, Bill, and Bill's wife, Julie. Can I get you two a cup of coffee?"

"No, no, thanks. We've already had several cups. And yes, I am Lieutenant Jameson, and this is my partner, Sergeant Gilmore. I'll get right to the point. I'm sure you folks are aware of the two missing Everglades City guys, Coombs and Coxwell. We would like to know what your relationship is, or was, with them and when was the last time you saw them."

Feeling like the leader of this gang I jumped right in.

"I assume you're aware that we had a run-in with them last year in the Caribbean. They were drug runners, and we happened to be in the wrong place at the wrong time. Thinking that we had stolen their drugs from some small island, they boarded our boat, and we had to disarm them and disable their boat to make our getaway. The only thing we damaged was their ego. We happened to run into them again at a bar one night and discovered they were with Bill's wife Julie, who had left Bill some time ago and ran off with the older one. We overheard them discussing their plans to get rid of her, and we had no choice but to rescue her before they could do her any harm. We could've done them in then. We had good cause. We left them in a precarious situation, but alive and kicking. I know it's a convoluted story, but it's the truth. We wouldn't have any reason to go after them again. I'm sure there are plenty of people who aren't very fond of them."

The Sergeant said, "That's some crazy story, but I want to know if you guys were fishing in the Ten Thousand Islands the same weekend Coombs and Coxwell went missing?" I didn't want to start lying quite yet. They may have cameras at the boat launch, and already know we were there. This could be a test.

"Sergeant," I said with as much confidence as I could muster. "We were there, only by coincidence. It's a big area as you know." Here comes the first lie. "We didn't see hide nor hair of them."

The Lieutenant said, "Those two guys may still show up, but it's not looking too good for them." I could see in his eyes that he had some doubts about our story. He thanked us for our time, and in their usual intimidating way, said they might have more questions for us later. His next questions will have to be long distance because soon we will be long gone.

We sat around the cafe for a while, not saying much, slowly wiping the sweat off our foreheads. We decided to leave the day after tomorrow. Frank still needed some time to figure out the route we were going to take. I told the guys to pack light. We can buy whatever we need when we get there. No need to overload the plane.

Whatever we had to do to get ready would have to be accomplished right away. We decided to meet at my place at dawn, *then off we'd fly into the wild blue yonder.*

CHAPTER 20

As planned, we met at my place at dawn, and thirty minutes later our Uber driver showed up to take us to the airport. George was there to meet us at the hangar, and the plane was outside and ready to go. Frank did a walk around with George making sure everything was visually in order. Frank had taken care of filing a flight plan with the FAA, which left us ready to go whenever we felt like it.

I handed George a money order for forty thousand dollars. He lit up like an atomic bomb. We loaded up the essentials we brought, planning on buying everything we'd need when we got to Alaska. We didn't have much, if anything, for cold weather clothes. Shorts and sandals wouldn't make it where we were headed.

I sat next to Frank in the front, and Bill took up the rear. I was hoping to get a little experience flying along the way. If something happened to Frank, someone had to be able to fly the plane. My nightmare from the other night was coming back. I thought I would be more suited for piloting than Bill, but that was just my ego talking. Since our encounter in the Ten Thousand Islands, my respect for Bill has grown immensely.

As we taxied toward the runway, Frank was in communication with the tower. We stopped at the end, and Frank turned the plane, so it was headed straight down the runway. I had a headset on also, and I heard the tower give us permission to take off. Frank immediately revved the engines with the brakes on. Within a few seconds he let off the brakes, pushed the throttle all the way forward, and I could feel the power of the engines hurl us down the runway. I was literally pushed back in my seat, and before I knew it, we were up, up and away. Wow, what a feeling of freedom! I think I just got over my fear of flying. We rose to about five hundred feet, banked to the left and continued climbing as we left Naples behind, and headed northwest out over the Gulf of Mexico.

We all took off our headsets, and Frank filled us in on the details of our flight plan.

"Ok guys, here's what I hope is going to happen. We'll be flying at ten thousand feet doing two hundred miles an hour. The furthest distance we can travel without refueling is fourteen hundred miles. We're going across the Gulf and into Texas, and we'll land just outside of Dallas in a small airport. That will keep us off the radar of these large airports. We'll fuel up there and spend the night near the airport. From Dallas, we go to Pagosa Springs, Colorado, then to Seattle and last stop is Palmer, Alaska.

"Hold on," I said. "What's with Pagosa Springs? Yesterday you mentioned something about Denver."

Frank continued on, "I heard about this place from someone back home, and I did a little research. It's a little east of Durango, close to the New Mexico border. They have some great hot springs there. The water comes out of the ground at more than a hundred degrees. We can stay at one of the spas, do a little soaking and relax a little. Maybe stay a couple of days. We're not in a rush. We'll get word to my cousin Pat sometime along the way of our change in arrival. I was told if I ever get out to Colorado to check Pagosa Springs out."

Bill and I, after a short consultation, decided *what the hell, why not?* Frank reassured us that we'd be better off to take the trip a little slow, that it made no sense wearing ourselves or the airplane out.

"We'll only fly during the day. Everyone will feel safer. We take four days, maybe five, to get to Palmer. The only problem will be the Palmer airport. It has a short runway, so we may have to land with the brakes on, and we'll be at the end of our fuel capacity."

"That's just great," I said, "At the end of our fuel capacity! Maybe we'll just glide in!"

Bill piped up, "Sounds wonderful, gliding into our last stop. I hope you've got your shit together, Frank. I'm not much of a glider."

"Don't worry Bill. I got it together, and I won't take any unreasonable risks. Just sit back and be happy and enjoy the view."

Flying over the Gulf of Mexico was an experience I won't quickly forget. I had never before appreciated its true beauty. You get a different perspective from this height. The indigo blue waters, stretching from one horizon to another, sparkled like sapphires in the sunshine.

I began to see oil platforms, lots of them scattered about below. From Naples, you never knew they were out here. Most people would rather not look at them. Out of sight, out of mind. We only heard about them when there was an accident and saw reports about the damage done by the oil. The Deepwater Horizon was the biggest oil spill in the world. Two hundred and ten million gallons of crude oil seeped into the Gulf. It made the Exxon Valdez look like spilled milk. It ended up costing British Petroleum (BP) forty-two billion dollars. Billions and billions of dollars were lost by the states surrounding the Gulf of Mexico and from the devastating effects to tourism and fishing. Tens of thousands of people's lives were in ruins. Twenty-two thousand people lost their jobs. Multitudes of claims were filed against BP and thousands of people were compensated, but sadly it was never enough to make up for what they had lost. There were also unscrupulous people that put in claims and won judgments who had never lost a dime from the accident. I personally know a couple of these people.

Money was flying around, some in the right direction and some not.

In the end, it all came down to negligence by BP. The pursuit of money at any cost. I guess you could say everyone was a little at fault. This lust we have for all the material stuff we don't really need. Unfortunately, it's all made from oil. I'm still not sure if there is such a thing as global warming, but I do know that the path we're on could harm us all in one way or another. I'm just waiting for Yellowstone to erupt. Then we'll have something to really cry about. A good mass extinction always clears the air. There are just way too many people; maybe that's the real problem.

About six hours after leaving Naples we landed at a small airport just outside Dallas. We refueled and got a room at some shit-hole motel near the airport. I did mention to the boys that with all the money we have, we could be staying in better places than this. Both Frank and Bill suggested I take it easy and relax. I still felt that Dolly Dimple Cabins wasn't up to the standards of three wealthy old geezers. Frank said, "When we get to Pagosa Springs we'll stay at one of the spas. A lot classier than Dolly Dimple Cabins." I was up for that!

The first day was pretty stressful for everyone, especially Frank. I now have total confidence in him. He was very professional, and if he didn't know what he was doing, he sure fooled me. He was Mr. Calm, Cool, and Collected.

CHAPTER 21

Early the next morning we checked out of Dolly Dimple Cabins and took off for our four-hour flight to Pagosa Springs. We had to fly over a part of the Rockies, and I was a little nervous about that. This would give us a preview of what Alaska would be like. Frank said we would have to increase our altitude to twenty-five thousand feet, but not to worry, the plane's cabin was pressurized, which makes it comfortable at high altitudes.

It's hard to imagine how much empty land there is until you get up in a plane and see for yourself. Every once in a while, we would go over a town or small city, but for most of the flight, there wasn't anything to be seen except mother nature.

Just about noontime, we landed in Pagosa Springs. Frank had the plane refueled and then we took a taxi into town. The taxi driver seemed to know everything, as they usually do. He suggested we stay at the Springs and Resort Spa. Well, who were we to say no?

As we pulled in, I could immediately tell this was not Dolly Dimple Cabins. This was a huge hotel, five stories tall and made out of rocks. All the rooms appeared to have big windows, and a private balcony overlooking the river. This is what I'm talking about! This is where the Three Old Geezers should be.

We paid the taxi driver and went in to see about a room. The lobby was big, and open, with two large fireplaces, one on each side. Couches, chairs, and rugs were spread around. There were little tables where you could play checkers, chess or some other card game. On one wall was the biggest television I had ever seen. It must have been ten feet across. A couple of people were watching Let's Make a Deal.

We made it to the counter and were met by a cute little chick, who Frank and Bill were drooling over, and I have to admit I was too. We asked what kind of rooms were available. She said the best room available slept six and had the best view of the pools and the river. She went on to say it was only six hundred a night. Before Frank or Bill could say anything, I said, "We'll take it."

We got the key, and up we went to the top floor. The room was enormous, with two bedrooms, a large lounging area, big screen tv, which I didn't care about, and the usual other amenities, like a bar and a gas fireplace in one corner, and of course our own hot tub. I opened the door onto the balcony, and sure enough, we had a room with a view. Snow-capped mountains in the distance, the river flowing by, and a sight of all the hot spring pools scattered around.

We quickly decided we needed a dunk in a pool, but first, we had to go down to the lobby to buy some bathing suits. We never thought we would need them on our trip. Finally, outside, we could see there were about twelve different pools. Some pools only held four or five people, and some were large enough for twenty-five or thirty. I was never very keen on taking baths with people I don't know, unless it was a woman. We had some information with us from the lobby, explaining the rules, and the differences in the pool temperatures. Some pools were slightly under one hundred degrees and ranged upward to about one hundred thirteen. The brochure also explained that these are sulfur-rich springs. You know what sulfur smells like. There was a hint of it in the air. The spring that fed this place was called the Mother Spring, rising up from the world's deepest geothermal hot spring. The spring water was so hot it had to be cooled before it was sent to the different pools. I had no idea how they kept the pools at different temperatures. I was impressed. A little footnote on the brochure stated that in Japan you had to go into hot springs without clothes. I happy I'm here.

We were ready to test our first pool. We thought we would try the hottest first. We were tough old geezers. There was a sign in front of the pool explaining the dangers of getting into water this hot. Death was one of them. I got one foot in and immediately understood what a lobster feels like when he first enters a pot of boiling water. We decided to start with the coolest one.

I also read in the brochure that people come from all over the world to this hot spring. They wanted to make sure you understood you were at a world-class resort, for medicinal purposes.

The minerals in the water supposedly can cure certain ailments. That's probably all bullshit, but I guess a good soaking won't hurt us and who knows, it just might help what ails three old geezers.

After about two hours of soaking away, and a few rum and cokes, our skin was spongy, and our fingers looked like white prunes. We decided to call it a day. We went in, showered and decided to go out to eat.

We walked downtown and stopped at Tom's Buffalo Corral. With a name like that it should be good. There was a short line made up mostly of young people. They looked pretty hip, so I thought they knew about this place.

Here we are out west, so I ordered a buffalo burger. It's got to be better than alligator nuggets. Frank ordered buffalo wings, and Bill ordered a scrod sandwich. I spoke up quickly and said, "Bill we're out west. There isn't a saltwater fish within a thousand miles." He changed his mind quickly and ordered a Colorado grass-fed ribeye. Just a note about scrod… Everybody thinks it's a baby cod, including every waiter or waitress and cook I've quizzed. I know the truth, and I got it from an old fisherman. He told me that SCROD stands for Ship's Catch Remaining On Deck. It's any whitefish that doesn't fit into a recognized category. I also read an article in a gourmet magazine that cautioned diners to eat somewhere else if they even saw scrod on the menu. I wouldn't go that far, but I wish people knew what they were being served.

We finished our meal, and I have to say it was pretty good, and went back to the room. We had a couple more Captain and cokes, and by nine o'clock these wild and crazy old geezers were fast asleep.

CHAPTER 22

We left Pagosa Springs early and took a straight shot to Seattle. It was a beautiful day, clear skies, a few puffy white clouds, and not a worry in the world. We quickly ascended to twenty thousand feet, and all was good.

I shouted, "Today's my birthday!"

"Wow! Happy Birthday!" both of them said in unison.

"How does it feel?" asked Bill.

"I don't know; I hate thinking about it. Honestly, I never thought I would make it to seventy. My father was sixty when he died. Died of cancer. I do know it will all end some day and that *someday* could be *any* day. My doctor told me that any man who makes it to sixty-five, no matter what shape he's in, has two out of three chances to make it to eighty-five. Even if that's true, at best I've only got fifteen years left. Having had three heart attacks, I should be dead already."

"Nah, you're too much of an old curmudgeon to die this young," said Frank.

"I am *not* a curmudgeon!" I protested. "You guys know me. I'm just a realist! Why is being realistic so often confused with being negative? I just tell it as I see it, and most people don't want to hear it."

"Yeah, usually it's best to keep your opinion to yourself, unless it's asked for. You know the old saying – you can lead a horse to water, but you can't make him drink."

"I know, and I'm working on it. It's my seventieth-year resolution, and you know what happens to resolutions. Anyway, it's hard to change an old geezer's ways."

Bill and Frank agreed with that one.

We flew on, each of us probably thinking about our upcoming destinations and what might be in store for us.

About an hour into our trip the engine started to sputter. It began as missed beats every now and then. Suddenly, there was a loud *Bang!* The sputtering got louder and more insistent. I anxiously looked at Frank.

"What the fuck is happening?"

Frank nervously said, "I don't know, but something definitely isn't right!"

Bill leaned forward in his seat and stuck his head between us and yelled. "Come on Frank, don't bullshit around! You're scaring the shit out of me!"

Frank's eyes were bulging now, as he stared intently at the instruments. "I'm not bullshitting anyone, just stay calm and be quiet. I need to concentrate!"

The engine was really making a racket now, and I could feel beads of perspiration on my forehead. I screamed at Frank to make sure he heard me. "Are we out of fuel?"

Frank yelled back, "No, we're not out of fuel! I don't know what's going on!"

After a couple more minutes of pure panic, the sputtering engines went silent, and so did we.

Frank was giving me his blank worried stare, and I was staring right back at him. I don't think either one of us in that second could think of a thing to say. It's that feeling you get when the unthinkable happens. It's like the feeling I got when I had my first heart attack. *No way! This can't be happening!!* It's called denial. Bill was saying something from the back seat, but we weren't paying any attention. All we could hear was the wind flowing over the plane.

I was finally able to utter some words. "Ok, Frank let's stay calm. What can we possibly do and where are we?"

"I'm going to try and start the engines again; I believe we're somewhere over Idaho. We can glide for quite a few miles from this altitude, but without a miracle, we're going to have to find a place to land." Frank got out the procedures for restarting the engines. He tried, but to no avail.

"Ok guys listen up!" Frank was taking charge. "Here's what we're going to do. We're already losing altitude, and when we get low enough, we're going to look for a place to land. A highway would be nice, or a field if necessary. There *has* to be something suitable down there."

I felt like I was going to throw up. I don't really like flying anyway, and the thought of crash landing was enough to give me another heart attack. My nightmare was coming back to me. Bill was quiet in the back, his brow pressed to the window, scouring the landscape for any possible landing spot. Frank tried to restart the engines again, but with no luck.

All three of us were sweating profusely and staring intently out the windows. After about five minutes certain objects became visible on the ground. We could see some large black animals scattered about. The terrain looked reasonably flat.

Suddenly Bill screamed. "There! Over there! Just off to our left! It's a dirt road - do you see it?!" We looked down and left, and sure enough, there was a narrow dirt road. I could make out a couple of trucks on it, and maybe some construction equipment.

Frank calmly said, "Ok, that's where we're going. This has to be done just right. There's no second chance!"

I said sarcastically, "I'm having a great seventieth birthday so far. Sure would be nice to see seventy-one!"

Frank carefully maneuvered the plane into position. We dropped lower and lower, and now I could make out some people standing around waving their arms. Frank whispered to himself, "I hope there aren't any telephone or electric wires around." I heard him, but said nothing. There was enough going on in my mind to worry about without adding to it. We continued to descend until we were within fifty feet of the ground. I must have closed my eyes because I don't remember anything after that until I felt the wheels touch down.

CHAPTER 23

It wasn't exactly a smooth landing. We bounced up off the dirt road at least three times before we finally came to a very dusty stop.

We all sat in stunned silence for a moment. Then all of a sudden in unison we exclaimed, "No money down and twenty-five years to pay, gotta get it while you can!"

Bill and I were whacking Frank on his shoulder and congratulating him over and over on his flying ability. As we were reveling in our good luck, there was a knock on the window. It was a guy wearing an orange hard hat, apparently some sort of a construction worker.

We all got out, and the worker said, "Wow! I've never seen anything like that before. My name's Jerome. We're out here in the middle of nowhere doing some work on this road, and you guys just drop out of the sky. Are you alright?"

I answered, "Yeah, we're ok, but here we are, like you said, in the middle of nowhere with a broken plane. Got any ideas?" He stood there with one hand on his hip and the other rubbing his chin, staring up at the sky.

A minute or two passed while he thought. "I have only one suggestion for you. I live around here, and there's not much going on for miles, but I do have a cousin who's a crop duster in the area, and he knows a lot about planes. I could call him and see if he can fly here and check out the plane, and maybe help you guys out of this mess."

Frank said, "That's a better solution that I can come up with. Let's give it a try."

Jerome pulled out his cell phone, typed in a few digits, had a quick conversation with the person on the other end, and then gave us the good news. "My cousin said he'll fly out here and check out the problem. He's a smart guy when it comes to planes and anything mechanical. He should be here in an hour if not sooner."

We didn't have anything to do except watch the buffalo wandering about, which I've never seen before.   It's hard to imagine a time when there were millions of them running all over the place out here.

About an hour later, the humming of a small plane could be heard. We all turned and to our surprise, coming right at us, was a double winger. The plane was only about ten feet off the ground, and we all fell flat. The plane went right over us throwing dirt and dust everywhere. I thought he was going to give me a haircut. As he passed us, he rose up sharply, did a barrel roll, came around and landed. He bumped to a stop not fifty feet from us.   The three of us were choking and spitting out dirt.

The pilot climbed out and shook hands with Jerome who had run right up to the plane's door hatch. The man was wearing what looked like a red football helmet, large goggles over his eyes and a scarf trailing down his back.

They came walking up to us, and Jerome made the introductions.

"This is my cousin, Jethro. Seems everyone in our family's first name begins with J. There's Jerome, Jethro, Joshua, Jimbo, Jenny, Jacob, and Jill."

I was worriedly wondering, how this was going to work out.

After shaking hands, Frank went with Jerome over to our plane to check it out. In a moment, they had the cowlings up on the engines, and were talking in what I supposed was weighty mechanical lingo. Frank got in and tried to start it again, to no avail. After a few minutes they walked back to us, and Frank said, "Jethro says the problem has to do with the fuel system. He's willing to fly me to get what we need and help us get her running again."

We were all relieved about that, and before I knew it, Frank was sitting in the back seat of the open cockpit bi-plane and taking off with Jethro to get the parts we needed. They took off and came right over the tops of our heads again. As I was swallowing more dust, I'll never forget Frank waving and smiling at us, as they headed off into the wild blue yonder. Jethro said they should be back in about two hours, so we had nothing to do but stare at the buffalo some more.

Sure enough, about two hours later, Jethro and Frank came roaring back and landed in a cloud of dust. Frank jumped out of the plane and yelled, "No money down and twenty-five years to pay, we got the part!" Bill and I were giving each other high fives.

It seems these crop dusting pilots know a lot about fixing airplanes. They're usually out in the middle of nowhere, and more often than not have to do their own repairs. Frank and Jethro worked for a couple of hours repairing whatever it was that was broken when Jethro finally asked Frank to get in and turn it over. I could hear our plane wanting to start, and after a few tries it farted, blew out some black smoke and began purring like a kitten. Bill and I jumped up and down with joy. I'm sure Frank was elated.

Frank charged the parts to his credit card, and we gave Jethro five hundred dollars for his efforts. He didn't want to take anything, but we insisted. Seems these country folk will roll over backward to do a favor for someone. We were greatly indebted.

We got back in the plane, Frank positioned us on the dirt road, and in a brown cloud of dust, we were off again. Right after we took off, Frank came back around and buzzed them. We were laughing our asses off. After all, w*hat goes around comes around!*

CHAPTER 24

After our harrowing experience, we finally made it to Seattle, or to be more specific, a small airport outside of Seattle. (Before I forget, I have to say that when I woke up this morning, I felt pretty good. I didn't have to get up in the middle of the night to pee. Maybe soaking in the hot mineral springs in Pagosa did me some good.)

I understand Seattle is a beautiful place, but we planned to make this a quick stopover. We arrived late at night. We were all exhausted from our plane trouble ordeal. After a bite to eat at some greasy spoon, we checked into a room at some less-than-desirable motel, and early the next morning we took off and headed northwest over the Gulf of Alaska towards Prince William Sound. Frank thought it was better and safer than going over the mountains. I had to agree. Landing in the mountains probably wouldn't have ended well, although a crash landing in the water wasn't a pleasant thought either. Bill was more than happy to stay away from the mountains since he was a Florida native and Florida is as flat as a fresh turd from a tall cow. Even a molehill seems tall to him.

We flew straight for Anchorage then headed northeast for the Matanuska Glacier, and the city of Palmer, where Frank's cousin Pat would pick us up. Hopefully Frank got word to Pat about our arrival time, since he had about a fifty-mile drive. It's a pain in the ass getting hold of Pat. You have to call this guy who calls this guy who delivers the message. Being out of touch like that might be a good thing though.

From our bird's eye point of view, the area was chock full of natural beauty. Snow-capped mountains, green forests, valleys, shimmering blue lakes, and rivers. About a half hour out of Palmer, Frank quietly said, "I knew it was going to be close on the fuel. I'm not absolutely sure we've got enough. We may be gliding in for a landing."

Well, that's all Bill had to hear. He screamed loud and clear, "You got us this far, and you run out of fuel in the last few miles? You've got to be shitting me!"

Frank calmly said, "Don't worry guys, this badass airplane can glide for quite a ways. You've seen how far we can glide. We can definitely fly on an empty tank; we just can't fly indefinitely."

"That's all very reassuring Frank, but what do you really think? No bullshit!"

A little smile came over Frank's face, and he laughed and said, "I was just kidding you guys. Nothing to worry about!

Bill yelled back, "That's not funny at all - you scared the shit out of me. I've been scared enough on this flight!"

Frank said he was sorry. To be honest, if I was confident enough to fly this plane, the thought crossed my mind to throw Frank out.

It wasn't long before Palmer came into view. It was a little airport, and from our altitude, the runway looked small enough to be someone's driveway.

"Are we going to land on that band-aid size strip of land?" I asked.

"Not to worry my friends, when we hit the ground I'll slam on the brakes, and hopefully we'll stop in time."

Bill muttered, in a slightly concerned tone, "I'm just going to take a deep breath and leave it up to you Frank."

Frank was on the radio with the tower, as we made our final approach. We flew around the airport once, just to check it out. There were mountains all around, and we swooped down along this long valley. We finally touched down with a screech of rubber, and rolled down the runway almost to the end, when Frank was able to slow enough to turn and taxi our way up to a ramshackle hangar.

We were met by a representative of the airport and Frank went inside to take care of airport business, whatever that may be. This was not a classy airport. The main (and only) terminal looked like a three-story chicken coop. There was a glassed-in room on top about ten feet by ten feet; I assumed that was the tower. Bill and I unloaded what little we had brought, and we sat by the plane in awe. Snowcapped mountains all around, deep blue skies, and air that smelled slightly of pine and freshly mown grass.

All we had to do was get the plane settled in and wait for Frank's cousin.

CHAPTER 25

We waited about an hour for Frank's cousin Pat to arrive. Finally, from across the parking lot appeared an old, olive drab military vehicle, with a big white star on the door. When I was in the army, we use to call these trucks a deuce and a half, which meant two and a half ton. It was used as a troop and cargo transport in WWII, the Korean War, and Vietnam. It's still used somewhat today. It sits high off the ground and has four sets of two wheels each in the back and two wheels in the front. Usually, there's a canvas cover over the back, but in this case, the rear was open. The front had room for two. I'm thinking, *is this what we're going to be riding in?*

In a cloud of dust, and flying gravel the truck skidded to a stop right in front of us and out jumped Pat. He was dressed in a sleeveless flannel shirt, blue jean shorts and some kind of half laced up construction boots. His legs looked as white as the mountain tops. (You notice these things if you're from Florida.)

It was only about fifty degrees out, chilly for us, but for him, it was probably a heat wave. He had a grin like the Cheshire cat, stretching from ear to ear on his round, friendly face. His eyes were wide-set and sparkled. His head was covered by shoulder-length thick brown hair. He was one rugged looking individual. He was stocky and at least six feet tall. Barrel-chested, with long, muscular arms. He didn't appear to have a waist, and his head seemed to be sitting right on top of his shoulders, where you would typically find a neck. He looked like a tall fire hydrant with a head and arms. If I had an altercation with some rednecks, I would want Pat on my side.

He ran up to Frank and gave him a big bear hug. He started jumping around and doing what looked like an Indian rain dance. I don't think he gets many visitors.

Frank calmed him down and introduced us. We shook hands, and I thought he was going to break a bone. He had a grip like a bear trap. Right away you could tell he was a personable, fun loving guy. I've been in business all my life, dealing with all kinds of people, and after a while, it only takes a second to scope someone out and make a judgment. I'm very seldom wrong. We all chatted a bit. He asked some quick questions about our flight and whether we'd had any problems. We didn't want to get into all that yet, so we kept the conversation short and sweet. We didn't want to hang around, so we quickly loaded what little we had into the truck. Frank got in the front with Pat, and Bill and I jumped in the back. We sat in an old car seat bolted to the floor, and off we went to Matanuska Glacier Outfitters to get whatever we needed.

CHAPTER 26

It was a typical sporting goods and clothing store, except for all the dead animal heads on the walls. There was also a lot of trapping equipment for sale, which you won't find at Dick's Sporting Goods in Florida. Alaska was like being on another planet, and people did things here that just weren't done back in Florida.

You had to have the right clothing to survive up here, and that's mostly what we were looking for. We bought heavy duty coats made out of the latest synthetic material, boots, gloves, shirts, pants, some fur-lined hats and of course, long underwear. I hadn't seen a pair of those in many years. I don't think Bill had ever seen any. Pat said we didn't need long underwear, but coming from Florida, the last thing we wanted was to be cold.

Now that summer was here, everyone in Alaska was lightening up and taking off their winter clothes, except for us, we were dressing for winter. We probably didn't need to buy such heavy-duty stuff, but we justified it, saying *if you get hot you can always take something off.* We spent about a thousand dollars each loading up on the latest and greatest. Pat also suggested we buy some sleeping bags because he didn't have much for extra bedding. We didn't care; we had a lot of money anyway. Bill also bought a couple of postcards to send to Julie. He said she liked getting letters in the mail. I thought he should just take a picture with his phone and send it, but I forgot that where we were going didn't have the luxury of cell phone service or WiFi.

We loaded up and took off wearing some of our new clothes. We were already feeling like back woodsmen. It was a beautiful sunny day, and we drove for about twenty miles when Pat pulled over and yelled back at us.

"Hey guys, this is where we leave the road and head off into the woods. We're going to take the scenic route, so hold on and fasten your seat belts."

I didn't know why we were leaving the road. We looked for seat belts, but of course, there weren't any, so we stood up and held onto the metal rail around the cab.

We turned off-road and bounced our way over boulders and across rivers that were two or three feet deep, and we weren't creeping along, either. It was all Bill and I could do to hold on. A few times our feet came right off the floor. We mowed down small trees creating a path as we went.

On each side of us were vast meadows sparsely dotted with trees leading up to the base of snowcapped mountains. I could have sworn I saw a couple of bears off in the distance. Alligators I'm used to, but not bears. We bounced along for what seemed like a couple of hours, but in reality, it was only about thirty minutes or so. We finally came to a screeching dusty halt right in front of Pat's cabin. I didn't waste any time getting off this circus ride.

CHAPTER 27

His cabin sat on the side of a mountain, overlooking a long valley which ended at a pure white glacier. The whole scene was framed by snowcapped mountains on all sides. The view was spectacular.

The cabin was made of logs and looked solid as a rock. It was about twenty by forty feet with a green metal roof. There was a large picture window on the front, facing the valley and glacier. A wide deck wrapped around this picture-perfect cabin. It was something you would expect to see in a travel brochure on the Alaskan wilderness. There were a couple of outbuildings off to one side. The smaller one was also made of logs and had a green metal roof. The other was a metal framed building about forty by forty with one large garage door and a green metal roof. There was a bulldozer, a backhoe, a 30-foot trailer, an old tractor from an 18-wheeler, and several unidentifiable pieces of equipment scattered about, one of which looked like a tank without a top.

I stood there motionless for quite a few minutes. The whole scene seemed to put me in a trance. I was almost at a loss for words but managed to pop off a few. "WOW! and I mean *WOW!* I don't think I've ever seen such a beautiful view. What's all the equipment for, and did you build all this yourself?"

Pat proudly said, "The cabin was made from lumber off my hundred and ninety-five acres. And, yeah, I did it all myself - well almost. I had some help from the neighbors. We help each other out. It's all basically made from scratch. In fact, if you guys had come a couple of months ago, you wouldn't have had all the comforts of home. Lucky for you guys I now have indoor plumbing and electricity. But my outhouse is still out there if you want to give it a try!"

I was trying to picture myself in winter taking a dump in thirty below zero. I guess you wouldn't waste any time. I'll bet there are no magazines in there.

Pat continued on, his words mixed with my reverie. "I have a construction business. That's why I have all the equipment. I clear land mostly and make roads for people. It's fun stuff, like when you were a kid playing with trucks in the sandbox, except these are big boy toys. Enough about all that, let's get unloaded and get you guys situated."

We got everything out of the truck and brought it inside. My first impression as I entered was one of warmth and coziness. The log walls inside were the same as the outside, a rich butterscotch color. The logs fit perfectly one on top of the other. There were some pictures on the wall, one, in particular, caught my eye. It was a picture of a bear shitting in the woods. *I guess that question is answered,* I thought to myself with amusement.

Also hanging on the walls were several different types of antlers from animals I couldn't identify. Near the entry was a large and very full gun rack. There was also a couple of bows and lots of arrows. I'm not a gun fanatic, but I do appreciate the feeling of power when you hold one. You could fend off a small invasion with this arsenal. The kitchen and dining area were on the left at the far end. In the middle of the room was a rather large black pot-bellied stove. Next to it was a 3 ft x 3 ft wood box filled with firewood. I bet it kept this place plenty toasty. In front of the stove on the floor was a large bearskin rug, or at least I figured it was. On the right, there was a big oak desk covered with papers, and I assumed this was his office. Further down, was a brown leather couch with another animal skin draped over it. There were a few other pieces of furniture of varying descriptions scattered about. Down on the far right was the bathroom. The door was open, and I could see the shower and tub. Thank heaven for indoor plumbing. Just after the couch and before the bath was a ladder leading up to the loft which appeared to be maybe fifteen or twenty feet long. I'm sure that's where Pat slept. Heat rises. To top it all off, there were two large picture windows with an unobstructed view of Matanuska Glacier. Who could ask for more?

Pat said he had three cots in the shed and we could set them up on the floor wherever we wanted, and that would be our sleeping setup. He apologized for not having separate bedrooms for us. He also informed us we would be having a special dinner in honor of our arrival, consisting of bear, elk and moose steaks, barbecued on the grill outside. I'm hoping they're better than alligator nuggets and frog legs, (although frog legs *are* pretty good... taste like chicken).

We settled in. Pat did his Alaska barbecue thing, and I have to admit it was one of the best meals of my life, with a view I will never forget. We had a few rum and cokes, and Frank gave his cousin a rundown on our flight up, our first adventure, and our last encounter which led us to escape to Alaska. Pat was pretty impressed with our exploits. He said he would have done the same thing, *except he wouldn't have been so kind.*

I'm pretty sure he would fit right in as the Fourth Old Geezer.

CHAPTER 28

I awoke the next morning about six, full of energy and ready to do just about anything. I could hear Pat outside chopping wood. Bill and Frank were in the kitchen making breakfast.

"Smells good! What are you guys cooking?"

Bill turned with spatula in hand and said, "You'll never guess. We're having leftover bear steak and eggs. You won't get that in Naples!"

"Sounds like the breakfast of choice up here," I said, yawning at the same time. "I can hear Pat outside chopping away. Doesn't he ever sleep?"

Frank spoke up, "I don't know what time he got up, but you have to remember there are about twenty-two hours of daylight now and you have to get things done while the sun shines. A lot of the year it's dark most of the time, and that's when you catch up on lost sleep."

I was beginning to remember what little I knew about the length of days way up here. I don't think I would fare well in the winter. I'm sure I would get cabin fever and suffer from light deprivation. I guess when you come from the Sunshine State, days of total darkness don't sit well, but I won't be here in the winter, so no worries.

I went outside while the boys finished making breakfast to say hi to Pat and check out the surroundings.

CHAPTER 29

Pat was standing outside, axe in hand, no shirt on, splitting wood. The sun was bright, though it was still quite early. I looked down at the glacier and had to cover my eyes. I made a mental note to find my sunglasses. It also felt pretty chilly.

I approached Pat, said good morning and asked him what the temperature was. He put down the axe and said, "Good morning! I see the last of the city slickers is up. It's pretty warm this morning - it's about forty-five degrees." He chuckled, "I would call it a heat wave."

"I wouldn't go that far," as I wrapped my arms around myself and started to rub my upper arms. "How much wood do you have to split, and why do it by hand? Don't they have machines for that?"

With a smile on his face, he said, "Yeah, they got machines for this, in fact, I have one, but this helps me stay in shape. When you can cut and split twenty cords of wood, you'll know you're in good shape. In fact, I'll let you guys have a go at it. Give you something to do. All of this huge pile of wood is for next winter, but it has to be done as soon as possible so it'll be good and dry come wintertime."

Just then Frank stuck his head out the door and called out, "Come and get it! Bear steak and eggs!"

After the delicious breakfast, Pat wanted to take us for a ride in the tank. I don't think it was really a tank, or maybe it was once. It had the tracks of a tank, a single one on each side, but that's where it ended. There wasn't any turret on top. The engine was hidden under an orange metal cowling in front, and I could see a couple of levers I assumed were for steering and a gas pedal. A couple of old car seats were bolted to the floor. I asked Pat, "What kind of contraption is this? It reminds me of an old German tank."

"It's not a tank," he said. "It's an old snowcat that was given to me by a neighbor. I took the top off, did a little work on the engine, and I use it to run around in the woods. It's especially useful in the winter."

I said, "Well it's quite the buggy."

He went into the shed and came out a few minutes later with four fishing poles and two rifles; one hung over each shoulder. I asked if we were going fishing or hunting.

He informed us in no uncertain terms, "We're going fishing for some trout or salmon for dinner, and the rifles are for protection." He sternly told us, "You never go outdoors without some firepower. Even if you go outside to take a leak, you never know what could sneak up on you and have you for dinner."

That's got to make you start thinking. I went back inside and got my .357 and borrowed one of his holsters. I felt a little better now.

We all got on board, buckled up and off we went, rocking, and rolling through the wilderness. I asked Pat, "Don't you ever take the highway when you go somewhere?"

He responded loudly, trying to be heard over the motor, "Not unless I absolutely have to. I like making my own roads as I go." Not much you can say to that. People up here apparently do their own thing.

After an hour or so of hurtling through the woods, we ended up at a beautiful river that was still running pretty fast from the spring snowmelt. We were in a valley which was lit up like a Christmas tree with early summer flowers. Patches of red, yellow, purple, orange and green, spread out before us like a giant quilt. The whole scene was surrounded by snowcapped mountains. I still get goose bumps whenever I think about it.

Pat helped us bait our hooks with fish eggs and gave us a little instruction. Throw the bait upstream and let it float down and be ready to set the hook. Seems easy enough. Living in Florida, we had all done some fishing, so we weren't rookies. The difference here was we were fishing for big silver salmon, not snook or redfish. We quickly noticed we weren't the only ones here. There were a couple of sizeable brown bear fishing upstream, which had me worried a little bit.

Pat said, "When you catch a fish, put it in this special bag." He was holding up what appeared to be a brown waterproof bag. "I'm going to keep it away from where we're fishing. It's not uncommon for the bears to come and try to steal the fish. The further we keep the fish away from us the safer we'll be. Fishermen have lost their lives up here by keeping the fish on them and being attacked."

Bill said, "I think I would rather have alligators around than giant bears. I don't think I could outrun one of those guys. Alligators can run pretty fast, but not for very long."

Pat said, "You shouldn't have any problems, but always keep your eyes and ears open."

We all got lucky that day, including the bears. We caught quite a few, but only kept a couple and threw the rest back. Just keep what you're going to eat. That was the motto we went by. It didn't take that long to catch what we needed, and within a couple of hours, we were our way back to Pat's house.

Fresh salmon for dinner!

CHAPTER 30

We'd been here six weeks already. Along with bouncing around the woods with Pat in his crazy vehicles, we've been fishing and elk hunting, although we weren't really interested in killing anything. Taking pictures with our cell phones was good enough for us. Pat shot an elk on one of our trips. He gutted it, skinned it, and butchered it right on the spot. He was a real mountain man. People in this part of the world rely on these animals for food. Back in the real world people get their meat all wrapped up nicely at the grocery store. Somebody else does the killing. Lately, I've been thinking about becoming a vegetarian. I saw a TED Talk on YouTube about the subject. The speaker said there are sixty billion animals killed every year and the average person eats over eight thousand animals in their lifetime. That's food for thought.

We did some hiking on Matanuska Glacier. That's something everyone should do once in their lifetime. Twenty-seven miles long and four miles wide at the end. It's like walking around on a cold, white, slow-moving moon. There are lots of hidden, very deep and dangerous crevasses which a person could quickly fall into, never to be seen again. Luckily, we had no such mishap.

We also chopped some wood for Pat, but that didn't last long. We each split for a few minutes which was all it took for blisters to appear on our hands and that was the end of that.

This morning we went into town to get a few things. Bill wanted to call Julie and see if anything was new; of course, I was curious about that. We climbed into the old army truck and headed off through the woods. I knew there was a real way, but we always took the road less traveled.

As soon as we got into Palmer, Frank went to find some cigars, and Bill immediately called Julie. After a few minutes, he came back to where I was standing by the truck and said, "You know, I sent Julie those postcards with information about our whereabouts in case she needed to get in touch with us. Well, she said she never got them. That strikes me as kind of weird."

"Oh, don't worry," I said, "I'm sure the post office screwed up, and they'll show up sooner or later. Send her some more."

"Okay…" He scratched his head and walked to the general store to get more postcards.

After our errands, we met back at the truck and headed back to Pat's. As we were bouncing along, I had a feeling of anxiety come over me. A suspicion that you know something, *but you just don't know what it is you know.* A foreboding you get when there's a big storm coming, or when someone close to you has been in a grave accident, and you haven't been informed yet. I had a premonition. I tried to put it out of my mind.

We made it back to Pat's, and I knew from experience it would take a few minutes for my stomach to settle back down. I never liked bouncing up and down.

We all pitched in and made an unusually interesting dinner. Squirrel and rabbit stew, with carrots, onions, potatoes, turnips, and a few more unidentifiable things Pat diced up. I thought it best if I didn't ask what they were. To top it off, Pat made his famous sourdough bread.

We took our dinner, along with a rifle, out on the porch. We ate our concoction while watching the green northern lights flow across the tops of the mountains. You could hear the wolves howling back and forth to each other. Pat told us that the wolves could be a problem, especially when they're traveling in packs. He'd had some confrontations, and had to fire shots at a couple of them. All I could say was *Wow!* The only thing that ever snuck up on me in Florida was a friend's cat.

After one of the best meals I've ever had, we indulged in some Captain Morgan, and Bill rolled a big, fat joint. Now that we're old and foolish, we sit around telling tales from when we were *young* and foolish. The stories seem to grow over time and take on a life of their own. Sometimes I wonder if some of them ever happened at all, and how many crazy things happened that I *can't* remember.

Before going to bed, Pat suggested we take a hike up the side of some mountain tomorrow, where we would have a great view of the glacier.

I'm looking forward to that. I know our time here is getting short. Sooner than later, we have to get back to the real world and deal with our nasty situation.

I still have some weird feeling nagging at me, in the back of my mind. Hopefully, it's nothing at all.

It wasn't long after a couple of Captain Morgans and a few tokes off Bill's giant joint that the Three Old Geezers and One Mountain Man were fast asleep.

CHAPTER 31

The next morning, we were all up at the crack of dawn. We were going to take our big hike today up the side of some mountain. Frank was making elk steaks and eggs. Pat was outside, doing who knows what. He was always doing something. He could never sit still. Frank, Bill and I could sit still forever.

We all ate our breakfast, except for Bill. He was moving around kind of slow and said he didn't really feel like climbing a mountain today. So, I suggested he stay behind and take it easy and keep an eye on everything.

We got all our gear together, and Pat reminded Bill one more time to never go outside without a gun. We took the tank this time and headed straight out into the woods looking for Mount Everest.

Pat found us a mountain to climb, which wasn't very hard since they were everywhere. We took the tank up as far as possible and hoofed it from there. Coming from Florida, the highest "mountain" I'd climbed there was about fifteen feet tall, which happened to be an old indian mound. I had climbed a few mountains in New Hampshire years ago, but nothing like this. It was invigorating and beautiful. We had sightings of bald eagles, bear, elk, and even a moose. We got pretty close to the moose, and if you've never been close to a moose I can tell you they are gigantic! Seven feet tall at the shoulder. A true miracle of Mother Nature. In fact, everything we saw from flowers, trees, and animals almost brought a tear to my eye. Words just cannot express the incredible scenery. An epiphany at every turn. I've been around people before who just don't seem to appreciate the beauty and wonder in nature. When you point out a flower, they say *what a pretty flower*, but they don't really see its innate beauty, and understand that the whole universe is inside that flower. I feel sorry for them.

We spent about two hours hiking upwards, before turning around and heading back down the mountain. We never intended to make it to the top. That was out of the question. We needed to be true mountaineers for that, and we were under no delusions. We just went up far enough to get an incredible view of the glacier.

We eventually made it back to Pat's cabin. Pat parked the tank near an old half-buried school bus that he camped in when he first got here. Now it was empty and slowly rusting away. There were plants growing out of the windows. It looked like a giant yellow flower pot.

We came around the side of the cabin and what we saw made us stop dead in our tracks, and we almost fell over each other.

There was a grizzly bear laying on the ground. Pat grabbed his rifle off his shoulder, not knowing if it was alive or dead. He slowly walked up to it and poked it in the head. No movement at all, and we could see a bullet hole right between its eyes.

I was yelling, *"Holy shit, what the hell happened here and where's Bill?"*

Frank ran to the cabin to look for Bill. A few seconds later he loudly called to us, saying,

"Hey! Look at this shit! I found this note on the door!" He brought it over to us, and we read it together. My heart sank, and my recent deep dark feelings of apprehension came to the surface. The note read:

> If you want to see your friend alive
> we're camped at the fork of the
> snake and moose rivers
> Come alone
> 8:00 tonight

CHAPTER 32

I immediately began screaming, "I knew it, I knew it! I had that feeling when Julie didn't get Bill's postcards! Those assholes from Goodland stole them from her mailbox and found out where we are, and now they have Bill! What in the hell are we gonna do?"

Pat came to the rescue. "Ok, let's calm down and figure out a plan. These guys came to the wrong place and fucked with the wrong people. They're way out of their element here. I know the location they're talking about, and it's only a few miles away from here. They want us to meet them at eight o'clock tonight, but first I need to skin this bear and cut it up and store the meat, or we'll have every beast in the world here before long including more bears."

Three hours later, Pat, had the bear done up and put away in a giant freezer in his shed. Looked like enough bear meat to last a lifetime. With his backhoe, he dug a deep hole and buried the remains.

We were in the cabin looking over Pat's weapons. Pat handed a rifle to me, one to Frank, he took one for himself and as much ammunition as we could carry. I also grabbed my .357. Pat selected a bow and some arrows.

"Why the bow and arrows?" I asked.

"It's a silent killer. You don't give yourself away when using it."

That made sense to me.

"Doesn't the tank make too much noise?" I asked. He made sense again when he replied, "They'll expect you guys to come up the main road which you will, but I'm going to head off into the woods, and stop far enough away so as not to be heard and sneak up on them from behind. You guys will take the army truck and do just what they expect. When you get there, I'll already be in position. I'll give you directions to the place. It's not hard to find. Obviously, we won't have the cover of darkness on our side since there isn't any, so we'll just have to do the best we can."

"Ok," I said reluctantly. "This all seems so risky. But I guess there isn't any other way of doing it. Poor Bill, I hope they haven't killed him already. I'm telling you these guys will never see the state of Florida again. I'm going to make them bear bait!"

A few minutes later Frank and I were in the truck ready to go, and Pat was in the tank. He gave the high sign and off we went. We looked like some crazy military convoy. We drove about ten miles, and then Pat pulled over and explained that this was where he was leaving the road and our destination was about five miles ahead.

Pat was in control. "Ok guys, listen up. There's a clearing where the two rivers come together. It'll be obvious when you get there. If all goes according to plan, I'll already be there and ready for action. Do whatever they tell you, be patient and wait for the opportunity. Hopefully, that's what I'll provide. So good luck and try to remain as calm as possible."

Pat went off into the woods with the tank, and we were to wait about half an hour. Time enough for Pat to get into position. Frank and I sat there worrying and wondering what was going to happen.

"Do you think we're going to have to kill these guys too?"

"I don't know Frank, but I'm not sure there's any way around it. These dumb-ass, redneck crackers aren't about to be reasoned with. They wouldn't have come this far just to chat. Just remember, whatever happens, shoot to kill." Frank repeated without hesitation, "Kill."

A half hour ticked by slowly. Then, just as Pat instructed, we started off for our rendezvous with these assholes. We drove pretty slowly; we didn't want to get there before our backup did. It was a dirt road, and you could tell it wasn't traveled very much. There were lots of ruts, rocks, and branches on it. I don't know how these guys found out about it. Maybe on Google Earth. Although I figured these dumb rednecks didn't know how to use a computer.

CHAPTER 33

Before long I could see ahead where the two rivers merged, and a small clearing was evident. I could make out a dark colored pickup parked right next to the river. I slowly pulled up within about fifty feet, and I could see Bill sitting on a tree stump, with his hands and legs tied and some blood on the side of his face. There were two guys standing, one on each side of Bill. One holding a rifle and the other holding a pistol to Bill's head. At a quick glance, I could see they were both of average height, wearing baseball caps, jeans and a couple of flowery Florida shirts, entirely out of place here. They appeared unshaven with a few days worth of beard. One had a beer belly, not easily missed. I told Frank to get out of the truck with his rifle, and I'd get out with mine, and I'd hide the .357 in my rear waistband. We both stepped out and stood behind our open doors.

I quickly said to these two douchebags, "You guys are making a big mistake you're going to regret."

The beer belly said, "Just shut the fuck up and drop your guns."

I retorted, "I don't think we're ready to do that."

"If you don't, my friend here is going to blow *your* friend's head off."

We didn't have much choice at the moment but to do what he said. They might be stupid enough to shoot Bill, which would leave them fair game, but they weren't the type to think things all the way through. I kept talking for as long as I could, hoping Pat was in position.

I nervously called out to them. "You guys have got it all wrong. We weren't responsible for anything that happened to your cousins, in fact, we don't *know* what happened to them."

The fat one quickly replied, "That's bullshit! You know *exactly* what happened and we're here to make it right! Don't make me tell you again, *Drop your guns!"*

At that very moment, I saw Pat at the edge of the trees in back, and out of view of these two dip shits. I was feeling a little better. I looked at Frank and said, "I guess we should do what he says." Frank had an even more puzzled look on his face than usual. I could tell he was scared. So was I.

The second we dropped our guns, the redneck holding the gun on Bill gasped loudly. There was an arrow sticking out of his chest, and he fell forward with a loud groan. His beer belly buddy looked to see what was happening, and in his moment of disbelief, I immediately grabbed my .357 from my back, brought it forward and fired, and instantly the fat redneck flew backward right off the ground.

I ran up as fast as my feet would carry me. I could immediately see the guy with the arrow sticking out of him was dead and the beer belly guy was moaning, ten feet from where I shot him. Pat came running out of the woods toward us. I said to him, "There's still one barely alive, and I'm gonna take care of him!"

I walked up to the beer belly, looked down at him and said, "You rednecks kill me, but this time I'm going to kill *you.*"

"Please…please." His weak voice was barely audible. "Just let me go. Please. I won't say a thing."

Well, I knew that wasn't going to happen. I quietly whispered to him, "You really fucked up this time along with your two asshole cousins, and it's coming to the same end. This is the end of your family tree. See you in Hell."

I fired once into his chest.

Frank quickly untied Bill. He was dazed, and in disbelief, but also visibly relieved.

I said to him, "What the hell happened, and how did they get to you?"

Bill weakly replied, "I'll have to tell you about it later. Right now I can't think."

"Ok," I said. "Later will have to do. At least you're still breathing."

CHAPTER 34

So, here we are. Two dead men, and a big mess we have to clean up. I hate this kind of shit. We never asked for any of this, from the two assholes in the Bahamas to the two assholes in Alaska. I really hope this puts an end to this family line of ding-dongs. I don't think we could ever explain this to the authorities and get off with a slap on the wrist. We had to get rid of these guys and their truck.

Pat yelled, "Ok, ok, we need to clean this area up really quick! Let's put these guys in the back of my truck, and we'll take care of them tomorrow. Their truck is another matter. We have to do something with it right now. There's a big lake about five miles up the road that one of these two rivers empties into. Let's drive it up there, take the plates off and sink it in the lake."

I said, "Ok, and did you look at their plates? These two dumb bastards drove their own truck all the way from Florida. Stupid is as stupid does. By the way Pat, that was one hell of a shot. Had you missed we may not be here now."

"Think nothing of it. It was my pleasure. Just like killing an elk, except I feel sorrier for an elk."

We loaded the two dead rednecks in the back of Pat's truck and covered them with a tarp. Pat said he would drive their pickup and we were to follow him. We drove a few miles up the road and came to a lake. After removing the license plate from their truck, we pushed it over a twenty-foot cliff where it slowly disappeared, hopefully never to be seen again.

As we were driving back, Pat suggested we leave the tank in the woods, and he would come back to pick it up later. We needed to get rid of these bodies. Bill wasn't feeling all that well, so I told him to wait till morning to fill us in on the bear and what had happened. We took the two rednecks, wrapped them in a tarp, and locked them in Pat's shed for the night. Pat said if we left them in the back of the truck there would be a pretty good chance they wouldn't be there in the morning.

I don't think any of us slept very well. We were up early with a single mission: get rid of the two bodies.

While eating a quick breakfast of coffee and toast, I asked Bill what happened, and what was up with the dead bear.

He started recounting the events. "I was sitting outside eating some toast with honey on it, and I heard a little rustling in the bushes. I looked up, and there was this huge bear snarling at me. I was scared to death. He reared up on his hind legs, and I was sure he thought I was breakfast. He started to charge at me, and of course, I remembered to bring a rifle outside with me which I quickly grabbed as I almost fell off the picnic table. I turned to face him, aimed and fired. Man, that was a shot I didn't think I could ever make. The bear fell about ten feet in front of me. I slowly walked over to him to make sure he was dead and the next thing I know I wake up in the back of a pickup truck with my hands and feet tied and an awful headache. As soon as those two jerks stopped the truck and dragged me out of the back I knew exactly what was happening. All they said was that this was going to be payback for what we did to their cousins, and that you guys would be showing up to rescue me, and that would be the end of us."

"Bill, relax. It's all over now." I said. "We'll take care of the rednecks and find them a final resting place. Pat has a plan, and we have to get right on it. You can stay here if you want."

Bill was adamant, "No way I'm staying here! I'm going with you guys. Nothing could keep me away from making these guys a permanent part of Alaska. I have no intention of staying here alone again!"

Pat explained his plan. "We're going to take my eighteen-wheeler, attach my trailer and load up the backhoe. I know of a very out-of-the-way spot, of which there are many around here. I'm going to dig a big hole with the backhoe and dump the two rednecks in it and bury them. Hopefully, never to be found."

Sounded like a plan to me.

We attached the trailer to the semi-truck and loaded up the backhoe. The two rednecks, wrapped in their tarp, were tied onto the trailer. We all got in the truck and headed out. We drove about twenty miles over dirt roads, and never saw a soul.

We got to Pat's secret location, unloaded the backhoe which he then drove off the road a couple hundred yards, and dug a deep hole about three feet wide, seven feet long and at least ten feet deep. We didn't want any animals coming along and digging them up. We dumped the assholes in, said a few nasty words, and covered them up. We spread lots of leaves, dead branches and anything else we could find on top making it virtually unnoticeable. It would be a miracle if anyone ever found these guys. We loaded up and headed back to Pat's as if nothing unusual had happened.

I felt a little guilty about what we had done, but that lasted no more than a second.

CHAPTER 35

In the two months we've been out here we've done a lot of exciting things, including killing two dumb rednecks. We've eaten bear, elk, moose, salmon, trout, squirrel, and other strange assorted wildlife. When Pat makes a stew it's best not to ask for a complete list of the ingredients. He was always shooting something and bringing it home. Most people in cities and urban areas in the lower forty-eight would think it was cruel killing all these creatures, but up here it was par for the course.

We have hiked all over the place, and my head is full of incredible views of mountains, forests, rivers, lakes, and glaciers. If we had wanted to go to the north pole, I think Pat would have been more than happy to take us. We decided that within a week we would say our goodbyes, and head back to alligator country and hope the police have forgotten about us.

Six days later, we were packed, leaving behind any clothes, and anything else we bought in Alaska that we wouldn't need in Florida. We left the same way we came, rambling along through the woods, with Bill and I holding on for dear life in the back of Pat's army truck.

After our bone-jarring ride, we finally arrived at the small terminal. Frank went inside to file our flight plan. Bill and I sat around for a few minutes letting our bodies readjust before loading up the plane.

Frank came back and told us it was clear for us to take off. We didn't waste any time. There were hugs all around, and Pat's final comment was. "Come on back anytime you want, but a little less excitement next time!" There were four thumbs up. I asked Frank if we could take a quick side trip and fly over the cabin and take a few pictures before we headed back. He was quick to respond. "No problem!"

We hopped in the plane and taxied to the end of the runway, and within a couple of minutes, the Three Old Geezers were *up, up, and away!*

CHAPTER 36

We were all in a rush to get back home this time. I trusted Frank a lot more now and said he could fly as far as he wanted, even at night if he chose to do so. We took a little bit of a different route going home. We wanted to see the Grand Canyon. We flew over it as low as we could, and the first thing that came to mind was, *that's a mighty big ditch!* You can't help but think about the history of the planet when you see something like that. It's incredible that a river could carve out that canyon. The millions of years it had to take, and it's still going on. There are those that say the earth is only six thousand years old. I'm sure they've never been to the Grand Canyon.

We got back to Naples in two days. After a long first day of flying, we stayed overnight in some small town in who-knows-where-ville. Frank did some flying during the night, and it was pretty cool, seeing the lights from small towns and cities. Frank even let me fly for a couple of hours. It's not as difficult as you think. We were in our own little world.

It was a beautiful sight as we flew in across the blue Gulf of Mexico, and the lush green of Naples came into view. We landed without mishap. It's hard to believe we've been this far and haven't damaged ourselves or the plane, except for the fuel nightmare. We had already called George along the way, so he was expecting us.

We rolled up to the hangar, and there was George directing us where to stop. Frank shut the engines off, and we all hopped out and kissed the ground.

George said, "I've been worried about you guys ever since you left. Everything is cool here, and I hope you didn't get into any trouble up there."

I answered quickly, "Not much really. Bill almost became dinner for a bear and we had to kill a couple of people, but other than that everything was pretty quiet."

"Oh sure!" George said with a smile. "You guys are hilarious! Well, you'll be glad to know everything has been normal here, thank heaven. Nobody's been snooping around looking for you guys."

"That's good to hear! If you don't mind, we'll leave you to your plane and call Uber to take us home."

George looked over the plane closely and asked Frank if there were any problems. Frank reassured him that the plane was in excellent condition and that he even got a few new parts to boot. He gave George a quick rundown on our near crash landing. I could tell he was even further impressed with Frank's piloting ability.

It didn't take long for our Uber driver to pull up, and before we knew it, we were back at my condo. We all agreed to meet as usual at Bad Ass Coffee the next morning.

I went inside my condo and quickly checked my messages, and sure enough, just yesterday, there was one from Lieutenant Jameson. Guess we got back just in time. He said he wanted to meet with us again as soon as possible. I called him right back. I told him, Frank, Bill and I had been out of town and just returned and that we would be happy to meet with him at nine the next morning at Bad Ass Coffee. He said okay and quickly hung up.

I called the boys and told them about the phone call and that we were to meet in the morning with the police. They weren't happy to hear that, but I told them to just be cool, and act like you don't know anything, and as much as possible, let me do the talking.

The next morning, we all met at Bad Ass, a little earlier than ordinary. I wanted to make sure we had our shit together when the police got there. I arrived and went inside to get my usual tree hugger breakfast. Frank was outside blowing smoke rings, and Bill was reading the newspaper. It seems nothing ever really changes.

We had a little chat, and it was decided *mum was the word.* I would do the talking unless they were asked a direct question. The fewer people putting their two cents worth in, the less likely we were to get our story screwed up.

At nine o'clock on the button a cop car pulled up in front, and Lieutenant Jameson and Sergeant Gilmore stepped out. The Lieutenant was tucking his shirt into his ill-fitting pants again, and the Sergeant had his usual flowery tie on.

They walked up to the table, and I stood up quickly and offered my hand.

"Good morning Lieutenant. Same to you Sergeant." The Lieutenant didn't look all that happy.

He spoke up. "I'll come right to the point. About a week ago a severed hand was found floating in the Ten Thousand Islands, and we were able to get a fingerprint from it, and sure enough, it belonged to one of the guys you had problems with in the Bahamas. We haven't found the rest of him, and we haven't located his partner, or their boat. Also, strangely enough, it seems their two cousins along with their pickup truck have disappeared too. Have you guys seen either of them?"

I spoke right up. "We haven't seen those guys since the Bahamas. And, no, we've never seen their two cousins. I can't imagine what happened to any of them, but from our experience with two of them, they probably had lots of people who didn't like them."

The Lieutenant continued on, "Where have you guys been recently?"

Careful in my reply, I said, "We've been in Alaska helping Frank's cousin do some repair work on his cabin. He lives on the edge of a glacier, and a recent storm caused some damage. You can get in touch with him to verify our whereabouts."

This time the Sergeant had his say. "We know you three were in the Ten Thousand Islands when the two Everglades City guys disappeared. It seems awfully ironic. Someday we'll get to the bottom of this. I hope you're not concealing anything from us because it'll cost you big in the end. If you know anything, now would be the time to tell us. This is looking more and more like a murder investigation. Now we have two more people missing. I suggest you three let us know if you plan on leaving town again."

"That's fine Sergeant, but I suggest you look at their drug connections. I'm sure that's where you'll find your answers." I could just tell he wasn't happy with us and didn't really believe what I was telling him. After a few more cautioning words they left.

Frank gave me his most worried look and said, "I hope this is as close as they get to figuring out what really happened."

"Listen," I said, "We can worry about this as much as we want, but the story has been told, and we can't change what happened. It just wouldn't be right if we got into trouble over all this shit. Let's try to put it behind us and hope for the best."

Bill piped up. "I agree. If it wasn't for those two assholes and their redneck cousins we wouldn't have anything to worry about. *We didn't kill nobody, and if we did, we didn't mean it.* We can use that line when we take our polygraph test. I love double negatives."

"It will never come to that," I said. "Let's just keep cool and let Mother Nature take its course."

No matter how cool we tried to be, we were still left to wonder and worry about the fact that we could end up in prison for something we weren't responsible for. We did kill four people, but it was all self-defense.

Sometimes I feel like a leaf floating down a river. Wherever the water takes me, that's where I'm going. No sense swimming against the current. Do I really have any free will, or am I like that leaf, just going wherever life wants to take me?

Hopefully, if and when this blows over, we Three Old Geezers can come up with another crazy adventure of our own invention.

Stay tuned!

ABOUT THE AUTHOR

Richard lives in Naples Florida. He is also a
singer-songwriter. You can email Richard at
rperron47@gmail.com

35741629R00091

Made in the USA
Columbia, SC
22 November 2018